"**Dinah, you gave me two weeks to find the man who's been threatening you. Can't you wait at least that long before making up your mind about us?**" Max asked.

She felt pulled in all directions. But the strain eased when she found herself nodding. "All right," she said. She sneaked a glance at him and, as always, was caught, unable to look away. "I don't mean to . . . dither so much," she murmured. "It's just that I'm afraid."

"Dinah, if you weren't afraid, you'd have no sense and no imagination. It's natural to be afraid after what you've gone through." He smiled, his eyes intent. "But you aren't afraid of me, are you?"

"No." It was an instinctive response.

"Good." His hands tightened on hers. "I hope you'll learn to trust me completely."

"I don't know if I'm capable of that," she admitted. "Or ever will be."

His hand caressed her cheek, and she tingled at the sensation. "Oh, you're capable of it," he murmured. He lowered his head, very slowly, until his lips touched hers.

WHAT ARE *LOVESWEPT* ROMANCES?

They are stories of true romance and touching emotion. We believe those two very important ingredients are constants in our highly sensual and very believable stories in the *LOVESWEPT* line. Our goal is to give you, the reader, stories of consistently high quality that may sometimes make you laugh, sometimes make you cry, but are always fresh and creative and contain many delightful surprises within their pages.

Most romance fans read an enormous number of books. Those they truly love, they keep. Others may be traded with friends and soon forgotten. We hope that each *LOVESWEPT* romance will be a treasure—a "keeper." We will always try to publish

LOVE STORIES YOU'LL NEVER FORGET
BY AUTHORS YOU'LL ALWAYS REMEMBER

The Editors

Loveswept® 595

Men of Mysteries Past

Kay Hooper
The Touch of Max

BANTAM BOOKS
NEW YORK · TORONTO · LONDON · SYDNEY · AUCKLAND

THE TOUCH OF MAX
A Bantam Book / February 1993

If you would be interested in receiving protective vinyl
covers for your Loveswept books, please write to this address
for information:

Loveswept
Bantam Books
P.O. Box 985
Hicksville, NY 11802

ISBN 0-553-44362-3

Published simultaneously in the United States and Canada

Bantam Books are published by Bantam Books, a division of
Bantam Doubleday Dell Publishing Group, Inc. Its trademark,
consisting of the words "Bantam Books" and the portrayal of
a rooster, is Registered in U.S. Patent and Trademark Office
and in other countries. Marca Registrada. Bantam Books, 666
Fifth Avenue, New York, New York 10103.

PRINTED IN THE UNITED STATES OF AMERICA

OPM   0 9 8 7 6 5 4 3 2 1

Great things are done when men and moun-tains meet.

—William Blake

Prologue

It was a fairly typical San Francisco night. Outside the penthouse, darkness hid the fog that had rolled in and now clung wetly to the city. Inside, antique furniture glowed in the soft lighting of several lamps. And in the sunken den, the brisk crackling of flames in the big marble fireplace was the only sound that broke the tense silence.

Frowning, the man on the couch stared into the fire, then spoke without looking at his visitor. "What makes you think you can catch him? So far, nobody's come close. A whisper of a name, that's all he is."

The visitor had prowled the room as he talked, but now sat in a nearby chair. Like his host, he kept his voice low. "With the right bait, you can catch anything. And anyone. The bait you have to offer is guaranteed to draw him out."

"It's guaranteed to draw every thief you could name out of the woodwork. They'll be tripping over each other."

"It won't be as bad as that. Tough security will weed out all but the—um—serious contenders."

"Tough security?" The man on the couch laughed softly. "We both know security's an illusion, even with state-of-the-art technology. Sure, the petty thieves will be discouraged, but it still leaves a fairly large field of hopefuls."

The visitor nodded. "I know, but there really aren't many ambitious enough to go after any part of the Bannister collection. It'd be damned difficult for any thief to unload something so well known and so priceless. The risk outweighs the potential profit. I really believe the bait would draw a *collector*, not just a thief out for a quick score."

"Some thieves *are* collectors."

"Not many. But the one we're after is. And look at his track record. Every piece we know he's taken in the last three years is one of a kind and has a colorful past, and most have so-called curses attached to them. Just like the Bolling diamond. One whisper that the Bolling is out of a vault and on public display is going to make his mouth water." The visitor shifted restlessly and added, "I don't want to risk the whole collection. This madman's greedy enough to take everything if we make it easy for him."

"I can't display the Bolling alone. It's part of the collection, and I've said publicly more than once I'd never exhibit any single piece alone. If I had a sudden change of heart now, any thief worth his salt would smell a trap."

"Dammit, I didn't know you'd said that. I can't ask you to risk the entire collection, it's too dangerous. A single piece I could protect, but if everything's together in one place, and he gets past me . . . he could get it all."

"The bait and the fish gone forever." Returning his gaze to the bright fire, the man on the couch said quietly, "It's taken my family almost five hundred years to assemble the collection."

"I know." A long silence followed, and then the visitor said, "It was a lunatic idea. I'll try something else, Max."

Maxim Bannister sent the visitor a wry look. "There's nothing else to try, and you know it. The kind of bait you need is rare. Offhand, I can't think of another collector who'd be willing to take the risk."

"I can't ask *you* to take it."

"What choice do you have?"

How happy is he born and taught,
That serveth not another's will;
Whose armor is his honest thought,
And simple truth his utmost skill!

   —Sir Henry Wotton
      The Character of a Happy Life

One

There wasn't much light, but he could see her clearly as she crept along the hallway. *Crept.* An accurate description, Max decided since she was moving with all the caution of someone who had something to hide. He was standing in the shadows himself, invisible to her, but he had a legitimate reason for being in the wing of the museum where his collection would soon go on exhibit.

Dinah Layton did not.

He watched her as she came nearer, and even though he was troubled by her presence here, he wasn't surprised to find he was interested in her in a far more simple and basic way. The truth was, he couldn't take his eyes off her. What little light there was revealed that she was not a woman who would ever be able to fade into the shadows.

Her hair was the vivid, true red that no bottled hair color would ever produce, and even under the faint illumination in the vast rooms and corridors of the museum, it gleamed with sparks of red and gold. Her skin was creamy pale and flawless, providing a stunning contrast to both her vibrant hair and the remarkable depth and clarity of her sapphire-blue eyes.

She was a beautiful woman, something Max had noticed the first time he'd set eyes on her. Nothing unusual about that, of course; he would have had to be blind *not* to notice her looks. Or to take note of how gracefully she moved and how innately sensuous her slender but richly curved body was—despite the fact that he knew she had lost some weight during the past couple of weeks.

None of which explained his obsession with her. Beautiful women had crossed Max's path on a fairly regular basis for twenty years and more without stirring his emotions into the kind of turmoil Dinah Layton had inspired. In general, he wasn't overly susceptible to physical beauty, and though he tended to make up his mind quickly about the people he encountered, that was a long way from becoming obsessed with a woman he knew nothing about.

As she came nearer, Max slipped back through the shadows, avoiding the clutter left by the workmen, never taking his eyes off her. She was clearly preoccupied, worried, or frightened. Her eyes seemed enormous in a strained, unusually pale face, and Max felt something inside him turn over with an almost painful lurch.

Big, sad eyes and a long, sad story.

Could it be that simple? Was his obsession with her really nothing more than his certainty that she was in trouble? His instinct was to help if he could, to aid rather than blame or judge or accuse—no matter if by doing so he risked something of his or even himself. Was that why he was here in a darkened museum long after the doors had been locked to the public? Why he was creeping around like the Shadow, watching her without giving his own presence away?

Or was he just fooling himself?

If he hadn't caught her, she would have broken her neck. There wasn't a doubt of that in Dinah Layton's mind. The museum was dimly lighted this late at night, and she was still a bit unfamiliar with the labyrinth of rooms, hallways, and galleries—to say nothing of the obstacles left by workmen in this wing. One such obstacle, a low stack of lumber, had caught her completely unaware, and she tripped over it. Since the lumber was half blocking the top of the marble stairs, she certainly would have fallen all the way down from the second floor to the first.

If he hadn't caught her.

He came out of nowhere, shocking her with his sudden presence as much as the rescue. He must have been close, but she hadn't seen him or any sign at all of his nearness.

"Careful." His voice was so deep and low, it was almost a growl, but there was a softness to it as well, and his powerful hands steadied her with surprising gentleness. "This is no place to be hurrying, especially in the dark."

As soon as Dinah got her feet under her, she pulled stiffly away from him, her heart pounding from more than the near fall. She recognized his voice, though this was the first time he'd spoken to her. During the past month—her first as assistant curator of the museum—he had been in and out of the offices near her own, which had been set up for the forthcoming Mysteries Past exhibit.

His exhibit, for all intents and purposes. He was Maxim Bannister, and he owned the Bannister collection of priceless gems and artworks that would make up that exhibit.

"Thank you," she managed in a somewhat stifled voice. "I—I'll be more careful." She wanted to edge away from him but stood her ground, looking up at his shadowy face with more steadiness than she felt.

He was an unusually big man, several inches over six feet and powerfully built, and would have been intimidating in the daylight and in innocent surroundings, but at night in the dimness of the museum, he seemed inherently dangerous. Not threatening exactly, but simply dangerous the way any man would be if he had a strong and forceful nature combined with uncommon physical size and the innate authority that came with having been taught early in life how to command others.

Still, despite all her chaotic anxieties and fears, and his imposing presence, Dinah felt peculiarly safe with Max Bannister. She might even have been able to relax, except for the small matter of her inability to explain what she was doing in a part of the museum where she had no business.

He had released her, but hadn't moved away. "You're working late tonight, Miss Layton." It wasn't a question, but something in his pleasant tone made it one.

Dinah was surprised for a moment that he knew her name, but then figured he probably knew every employee of the museum by name. In fact, he probably knew a great deal more. The security arrangements for his upcoming exhibit were extremely detailed, and no doubt included background checks on museum employees. A little chill chased down her spine at the realization.

God, why hadn't she thought of that before? If she had, she might not have taken this job, and if she hadn't taken the job, then maybe none of it would have happened. . . .

"Paperwork," she said as steadily as she could, answering his implied question. "There's so much of it with all the construction and the new exhibit, and . . . I want to do a good job here."

If he wondered what paperwork she could possibly have been doing so far from her office and in the wing that was closed off while it was being readied for his exhibit, he didn't ask. Instead, he took her arm firmly and began leading her down the wide marble stairs.

"It's after eight, Miss Layton, and Ken doesn't

expect his assistant to put in such long hours," he said, referring to Kenneth Dugan, the museum's curator. "Besides, the security guards are a little jumpy these days, and would rather have none of us spend our evenings wandering the halls."

Dinah's impulse was to immediately apologize—give way, give in, avoid any kind of conflict—but she fought off the urge. It was more difficult than it had been a month ago, and cost her in added stress, but she managed.

"Because of the robbery last week at the modern art museum, you mean?" she asked, keeping her tone as casual as his.

"Partly, yes." They had reached the bottom of the stairway and, still holding her arm, he paused momentarily and glanced down at her before turning to cross the lobby toward the hallway of offices on the far side. "I'll wait while you lock up your office," he added.

"That really isn't necessary, Mr. Bannister. I have a few more minutes' work, and—"

"Work for tomorrow." His tone remained pleasant. "You've been here nearly twelve hours, and you didn't take a break for lunch. I think your day's been long enough, Miss Layton."

Dinah felt another little chill. She had been told that Max Bannister never missed a thing, but how did he know she'd been here all day? She hadn't seen *him* today, not until he'd caught her on the stairs.

The security guard at his desk in the lobby looked up but didn't challenge them as they passed. Dinah doubted that her companion was challenged very often by anyone in any situation, and he certainly had the run of this museum no matter what the hour. In fact, he could do pretty much what he wanted to. She wondered vaguely what it was like to walk through life like that, sure of yourself, unafraid, able to command resources other people couldn't even comprehend.

Safe.

They were now in the well-lit hallway where the offices were located. She sneaked a glance up at his ruggedly handsome, rather hard face, and swallowed with difficulty. He was incredibly wealthy and, though he kept a low profile, he was financially and socially powerful in San Francisco. Rumor had it that he was a wonderful friend and a very bad enemy. She knew she wouldn't want to cross him in any way.

As soon as they reached her office, she went across the small, windowless room to her desk to get her purse and coat. He remained by the door, both unnervingly large and imposing in his dark raincoat, and she was conscious of his steady gaze on her. She could still feel the light grip of his hand on her arm, as if he had marked her somehow.

"I'll take you home," he said.

Dinah had just taken her coat off the wooden coat tree, and swung around to look at him in surprise. His steel-gray eyes were unreadable. She hoped her own were, but was very much afraid they showed the alarm she felt. She would have been grateful for a ride from almost anyone else, but with him she felt nervous, tense, and guilty. The last thing she wanted was to be alone with him in a car.

"Thank you, but that isn't necessary," she said hurriedly. "I live only a few blocks away, and this is a safe neighborhood. I always walk."

He shook his head slightly, his eyes never leaving hers, and repeated, "I'll take you home." There was nothing autocratic or commanding in his tone, yet something in it didn't invite argument.

She looked away from his unreadable gaze and began to shrug into her coat. He immediately took three steps into the room and held the coat for her, a gesture of courtesy that was quite probably impersonal, she told herself, even though she couldn't help stiffening. And she jumped when his warm fingers touched her neck as he gently drew her long hair over the collar of the coat.

Calm down! she urged herself silently as she got her purse from the desk. The advice only half worked, but half was good enough for the moment. She was able to turn out the lights in her office and lock the door without fumbling while he stood by silently. She even managed not to jump again when he took her arm and led her back down the hallway.

He released her long enough to sign them both out in the security logbook, speaking pleasantly to the guard at the desk, then took her arm again. Another security guard was passing through the lobby on his rounds, and let them out with a polite good night, addressing them both by name. His smile was approving, which baffled Dinah until she wondered if the guards had told Bannister she'd worked very late every night for more than a week. If that was the case, he might have remained late tonight himself to check on her.

But why? It was, strictly speaking, no business of Max Bannister's if she chose to work until midnight. He didn't own the museum—at least, she didn't think he did—and had nothing to do with the running of it, barring the arrangements for his own exhibit.

Grappling with the uneasy thoughts, she barely noticed the chill wind outside. Silent, she got into the passenger seat of the Mercedes parked at the curb when he opened the door for her. When he got behind the wheel, she offered directions to her apartment building and then fell silent again. She couldn't seem to come up with any small talk.

The sedan drove almost noiselessly, the engine purring, and inside it was so quiet that Dinah jumped slightly when he spoke, even though his voice was still low.

"You haven't been in San Francisco very long, have you, Miss Layton?"

She shot a glance at him, but it was too dark to see his face clearly. Every time they passed a streetlight, however, she could see his hands on the steering wheel. They were large hands, almost brutally powerful, and yet they were beautiful, too, and she felt no fear of them. Odd. That was very odd, she thought.

Clasping her own hands tightly together in her lap, Dinah finally answered him. "No, not long. A few months."

"Where are you from?"

The question was probably an innocuous one, and was certainly asked in a casual tone, but it nevertheless caused more tension to seep into Dinah's body. She was tempted either to be vague or to lie outright, but when she replied she wasn't surprised to hear herself give him the truth. There was just *something* about him, something that evoked honesty.

It was a bit frightening.

"Boston," she murmured.

"Is that where your family is?"

A traffic light had halted them, and Dinah stared at it. One of Murphy's laws, of course: If you wanted to get somewhere in a hurry, every light would stop you. Not that she was in a hurry to get home, what she wanted was to get away from Max Bannister's so-casual questions.

"Miss Layton?" He was looking at her. She could feel it.

In the most neutral, indifferent voice she could manage, Dinah said, "I don't have much family. An older brother. He lives in Boston with his wife and kids."

After a moment, Max said, "I gather you two aren't close."

"You could say that." She felt a flicker of relief

when the light changed, and added quickly, "The light's green."

The Mercedes moved forward smoothly, and his attention was once more fixed on the road. But he startled her by murmuring, "I'm sorry you're uncomfortable with me."

If she had been thinking clearly, Dinah would have met that statement with silence, allowing him to believe it. But she wasn't thinking clearly. At least, that was what she told herself when she heard her surprising response.

"It isn't that. I mean . . . I just don't know you."

"Then there's hope." Before she could respond to the lightly spoken words, Max added, even more lightly, "I really can't help it if I look like a thug, but I can assure you it's a deceptive appearance. I can even produce quite a few references attesting to my character, if it'll make you less wary of me."

"That isn't necessary." Her voice was a little stiff, and she stared straight ahead at the second traffic light to halt them. She didn't understand why he was talking this way. Why would her opinion of him possibly matter to him?

"I think it is." His voice was quiet now. "I don't want you to be wary of me."

Dinah felt the cold touch of panic, and couldn't entirely hide the strain when she spoke. "Mr. Bannister, since I have nothing to do with the exhibit of your collection, there's no reason why you should concern yourself with my feelings."

"In other words, I should mind my own business?" he said wryly.

Something in his tone made heat rise in her cheeks, and she felt absurdly defensive. "The light's green," she muttered.

He didn't speak again until he pulled the car to the curb before her apartment building.

"I wish you could trust me."

It was almost a plea, and it unnerved Dinah more

than anything he'd said. What did he mean? How much did he really know? And why did she suddenly want to cry? This man was a *stranger,* for God's sake. How was he able to arouse such strong reactions and emotions in her?

Struggling to hold on to her composure, she ignored his appeal because she didn't know how to respond to it. "Don't bother to get out, please. Thank you very much for the ride, Mr. Bannister." She didn't give him a chance to respond, but immediately got out of the car and hurried up the sidewalk to the well-lit entrance. The car remained at the curb, she knew that, but she didn't look back.

Max stared at the building for some minutes after she'd gone inside, then allowed his gaze to track upward to the second floor, where he knew her apartment was. There had been a light on when they arrived, and now other lights came to life behind drawn curtains. Feeling unusually restless, he tapped his long fingers against the steering wheel as he watched her windows for a moment. A slight frown pulled at his brows. Slowly, he scanned the building from one corner to the other. At the far corner, he caught a glimpse of movement and the blink of a pencil flashlight. Relaxing slightly, he put the car in gear and drove away heading for his own apartment.

When he got home he sat before a blazing fire in the marble fireplace, as he had months before when he had first agreed to risk his collection. But this time he wasn't thinking of his priceless heritage.

Big, sad eyes and a long, sad story. It was a joke among his friends, a catch phrase meant to remind him that sometimes sad eyes were calculating, and some sad stories had little basis in fact. It had been years since his compassion had proven to be wasted, but his friends were good ones and they worried still.

Max knew that. But he trusted his instincts, and his instincts told him Dinah Layton was in trouble.

The problem was, his heart was telling him even more. There was no question this time of objective compassion.

Miss Layton. He'd made a point of addressing her that way, even though he'd been thinking of her as Dinah from the moment he'd first seen her. He had spent more time than necessary at the museum this last week, simply because he had hoped to find an opportunity to talk to her. The opportunity hadn't arisen until tonight; each time he'd found some excuse to speak with her, Ken Dugan had appeared out of nowhere before Max could get near her office, eager to help with the "problem."

Max reflected now that Dugan was a good man; he was also ambitious, and clearly assumed that getting in good with Max Bannister could benefit him on some future day when he might need a favor. He certainly wasn't the first to believe that, and he wasn't wrong. But his timing was lousy.

Max shifted restlessly on the couch and frowned, accepting the fact that his own timing wasn't the greatest. Especially when the lady who was beginning to haunt his every thought quite obviously had secrets of her own.

"Why were you in the exhibit's wing tonight, Dinah?" he murmured to himself as he stared into the fire. "What are you afraid of?"

Dinah looked at the ringing phone for several moments, terrified of answering, more afraid not to. It wouldn't do any good not to answer, she knew. The last time she had ignored his call, he had left her a message: A single, wilted lily outside her door. That had been more frightening than the phone calls, because it had reminded her of how easily he could get to her. How close he had been. Just outside her door . . .

She picked up the receiver with icy fingers, then said, "Hello?" in little more than a whisper.

"You did very well tonight, Dinah." His voice was low, without emotion. Indistinct and anonymous, it could have belonged to any man—or only one man. It was a voice she'd heard in her nightmares for nearly two years.

"Leave me alone. Please, leave me alone." Her own voice was a thin thread of sound, stretched taut by hopelessness.

He chuckled. "You know I can't do that, Dinah. There are things I want you to do for me. The way you did tonight. You did fine, just fine. It earned you a reprieve. If you go on being a good girl, I might even disappear from your life forever. But if you aren't good, Dinah, you know what I'll do to you. Do I have to tell you again?"

"No," she answered, the sick threats and promises he had made echoing inside her head, tangling with the dreadful memories she couldn't escape.

"I'm glad we understand each other. You just go on being a good girl and do as you're told, and I won't have to hurt you. The way I did before."

Dinah's fingers were so icy and numb, she dropped the receiver a few moments later when she tried to put it back on its cradle. On her third try, she got it into place. Then in the brightly lit living room, she sat in a chair in a corner so she wouldn't have to keep looking over her shoulder. Legs drawn up, her eyes moving around ceaselessly, she could see the double-locked front door and the closed windows. The silence was loud, and she listened with all the rigid alertness of a hunted animal for an alien sound.

Dawn was hours away.

Though he had no reason connected with the exhibit for going, Max arrived at the museum early the next morning, before it was even open. He knew there was something wrong when a guard let him in; the worried expression on the man's face told him that. Max didn't question him, however. He stepped into the lobby and stood gazing around, taking note of the unusual activity and the fact that the night guards were still present, two of whom were standing near the offices talking to Ken. Dinah was there also, though she didn't seem to be saying much.

Before Max could approach them, Morgan West, clipboard in hand and clearly upset, crossed the lobby toward him. She was the director of his forthcoming exhibit, a position of responsibility for which she seemed too young. Her long black hair was pulled back casually in a ponytail, the style emphasizing the fine bone structure of her face, and the gold sweater she wore over dark slacks clung lovingly to a set of measurements that drew a guard's admiring and wistful attention.

Max waited until she reached him before quietly asking, "What's up?"

"Maybe a tempest in a teapot," she replied in her vibrant, musical voice. "Then again, maybe not. When the morning guards came on duty, they found an open door, Max."

"Which door?"

"In the back, one of the service entrances. The one near the basement."

After a moment of thought, Max said, "The door farthest from any of the museum's exhibits."

"Yeah. Peculiar, isn't it? If anybody wanted to break in, why would they choose an entrance so far from anything of value? Especially since they'd have to get through at least three corridors protected by laser alarms."

The security devices Morgan spoke of were activated after the museum's doors were locked to the public. The guards, senior employees, Max, and Morgan all had magnetically encoded cards enabling them to shut off corridor sensors when they needed to pass through. Only the head curator had the code that shut off security devices protecting individual exhibits.

"I gather nothing was taken?" Max asked.

"As far as we can determine, nobody came in," Morgan replied. "The door was ajar, but not a single alarm was tripped. And since the new computer isn't on line yet, we have no way of knowing if anyone used a security card for that corridor, or when. But the door alarm was deactivated—from inside."

Max had donated to the museum a computerized security system that would, among other things, provide a log of all alarm shutdowns, but it was still being installed. The existing system, while a relatively good one, allowed anyone with a security card to deactivate corridor alarms and sensors at will and leave no record of when and where it had been done. As for door alarms, they were individually coded because so many of the staff had to be able to get in and out without leaving all the doors unlocked.

Slowly, Max said, "So unless someone accidentally forgot to reactivate the door alarm earlier in the day, one of us could have used a security card to get through the corridor and open it sometime later. But why? Why leave the door ajar but the corridor alarms active?"

"It doesn't make sense," she said, clearly worried. "You think somebody might be testing our security?"

"It's a possibility. Have you talked to Wolfe?"

"He's on his way in." She grinned suddenly. "And you should have heard his language when I called him. I don't think I woke him up, but I have a feeling he wasn't alone."

"He seldom is," Max said dryly. He glanced around and spotted Ken approaching with a frown. In a lower voice, he said, "Morgan, do me a favor and occupy Ken for a while, will you? If he starts in on explanations and reassurances, I'll be here all day."

"Sure, boss." Her large amber eyes held a gleam of amusement. "She went back to her office, by the way."

"Who?" Max asked, his pretense of ignorance unconvincing even to him.

"Dinah." Morgan lifted an eyebrow, then took a few quick steps away to intercept the head curator. "Ken! Just the man I want to see. We're having a few problems installing those pressure plates for the exhibit, so if you could take a look?"

"But, Morgan, I wanted to talk to—"

"It's *very* important we get those plates right, Ken, and you're so good with things like that. It'll only take a minute, I promise. Max'll be around for hours, you can talk to him later. Nice suit. It brings out the color in your eyes."

"Thank you, I'm glad you like it, but—"

Smiling a little, Max watched the flustered, flattered, and thoroughly controlled Ken being led away. Morgan despised being treated like a bosomy nitwit, but she was too intelligent not to use her figure and big, kittenlike eyes to good effect when necessary. She was also damned observant, Max thought. Or had he merely been wearing his heart on his sleeve?

Pushing that disturbing possibility out of his mind, he turned and went toward the hallway of offices. What was he going to say to her? At first, he had considered her merely shy, but gradually realized she was afraid. Now, despite what she had said in the car the night before, he knew she was afraid of him as well as something else.

He was aware that he could both look and sound forbidding, which was why he'd mentioned it somewhat mockingly to Dinah, but he certainly hadn't intended to come across to her as threatening. Given time, he hoped he could convince her he wasn't an ogre—but time might prove to be a luxury he couldn't afford.

Dinah had been somewhere she shouldn't have been last night: The exhibit's wing. And although that section was nowhere near the door they'd found open this morning, the question of what she'd been doing there remained. Since the background information she'd provided the museum was so sketchy, and since she'd made it a habit to work late hours unsupervised, Dinah looked suspicious even to Max who very much wanted to believe in her.

Which meant that Max had to find out the truth about Dinah before she ended up at the top of everybody's list of suspects. The question was, how could he persuade Dinah to confide in him without adding to her fear?

He hesitated in the open doorway of her office. She was at her desk, gazing down at a stack of papers on the blotter—and if ever guilt was written on anyone's face, it was written on hers.

He knew then she had opened the service entrance door.

"Good morning," he said quietly.

She looked up with a start, so unnaturally pale that the only color in her face was the dark, haunted sapphire of her eyes. She didn't say a word, just stared at him, frozen.

There were so many questions he needed to ask her. So many. "Miss Layton—" He stopped, shook his head slightly at the ridiculous formality, then began again. "Dinah, do you believe in love at first sight?"

Two

If nothing else, his words wiped the fear out of her eyes. "I—I beg your pardon?" she ventured hesitantly.

"It's a simple enough question." He came into the office and sat down in a visitor's chair, smiling at her across the desk. "Do you believe in love at first sight?"

"Mr. Bannister, I—"

"Max, please."

Clearly baffled, and not a little wary, she half nodded but didn't address him by name. "No, I don't believe in it."

"Any particular reason?"

"Because it isn't possible. You can't love someone you don't even know, it's absurd."

"I used to think that," he said. "But when an impossible thing happens to you, it's a little absurd to go on calling it impossible, don't you think?"

Dinah's expression asked silently why on earth he'd brought up the subject, but she didn't say it. She merely shrugged. "I suppose."

"So you do agree that some things are impossible only because we haven't experienced them yet?"

She stared at him for a long moment and then,

with a touch of dryness in her voice, replied, "Philosophically speaking, yes, I do agree with that."

"Good. Have lunch with me."

Instantly, the wary look returned to her eyes. "Thank you, but I have a lot of work to do."

"Dinah, this museum won't fall into ruins if you take an hour off for lunch."

"I know that," she said a little stiffly. "But I prefer to work through lunch, Mr. Bannister."

"Max," he corrected. "Please."

"If you insist. Max."

Max didn't lose his smile, though it took effort. He wanted to remain and find a way through her wall of reserve, at least convince her to have lunch with him, but he caught the distant sound of a voice he recognized. At the moment, he judged it was more vital to intercept Wolfe. Getting to his feet, he went to the door and then turned back to look at her.,

"Are you afraid of me, Dinah?" he asked quietly.

A hint of rose came and went in her cheeks. "How could I be afraid of you. I don't know you."

"That's what I was wondering." He paused a beat, then added, "Don't work too hard." Without waiting for a response he was pretty sure he wouldn't have gotten anyway, he headed down the hallway toward the lobby.

About two steps from the hall, he effectively but unobtrusively blocked Wolfe's passage. "You look grim," he noted mildly.

"I'm not exactly happy," Wolfe Nickerson agreed. At thirty-six, he was two years younger than Max. They were half brothers, raised by their fathers on opposite coasts of the country, and had gotten to know each other well only as adults. But even though their knowledge of each other went back less than fifteen years, there was an unusually strong bond between them.

Physically, they didn't look alike at all—except that both were well above medium height. Wolfe was about six feet tall, with powerful shoulders and was obviously athletic. He had thick auburn hair, steady blue eyes, and a charming smile that drew women like a magnet. He also shared with Max a low, deep voice, but his had a menacing edge to it sometimes. Like now.

"Any ideas about that open door?" Max asked.

"Just one. According to the guards, Dinah Layton's been wandering around the museum after hours, including last night. I'm going to talk to her now."

"Talk to me first," Max suggested. He took Wolfe by the arm and turned him toward the main entrance of the museum.

As soon as they were outside at the top of the wide steps, which were deserted that early in the morning, Wolfe stopped. "Max, what the hell is going on? It's barely dawn, it's freezing out here, and I haven't had my coffee."

"I'll buy you a cup," Max said. "There's a café around the corner."

Wolfe didn't move. Standing there with the collar of his black leather jacket turned up and a scowl on his face, he looked more like a ruffian than a security expert and representative of Lloyd's of London. "Morgan didn't roust me out of bed so you could buy me coffee. What's up, Max?"

Max slid his hands into the pockets of his coat and debated silently for a moment. Then he sighed. "You think Dinah may have opened that door?"

"Yes, I do," Wolfe replied flatly.

Calmly, Max said, "I'm reasonably sure she did."

Wolfe blinked. "Okay, so why did you cut me off when I was going to question her?"

"Because she's scared."

"If you were a thief's accomplice, you'd probably be scared too," Wolfe said. "So what? She's a hell of a lot more likely to talk if she's rattled."

Max shook his head slightly. "Wolfe, have you ever

seen genuine terror in someone's eyes? Or the trapped look of a hunted animal?"

"Once or twice." Wolfe wasn't scowling any longer. Instead, he studied Max thoughtfully. "I gather we're still talking about Dinah Layton?"

"Yes. You've spent most of your time these last weeks dealing with the security company, so you haven't been around the museum very much. But I have. Dinah seemed a bit nervous when she first came to work here about a month ago. Understandable since she was new to the job and didn't know any of the people here, and the place is in an uproar getting ready for the forthcoming exhibit. Then, about three days later, nervous became scared. Over the past few days, scared became terrified. *If* she opened the door, it was because she was forced to."

"Blackmail?" Wolfe offered. "I was going to tell you today that the background check I ran on her has more holes in it than Swiss cheese. Maybe she has a secret someone's holding over her head."

Max thought about it briefly, then shook his head. "I don't think so. That look in her eyes . . . I've seen something like it in trauma victims. She's been hurt, and she's been terrorized. I think someone's threatening her physically."

Crossing his arms over his broad chest, Wolfe brooded for a moment. "Okay, when it comes to people, your intuition's better than mine. Maybe you're right. But we still need to know for sure, and we need to know who's pulling her strings. I have to talk to her."

With a faint smile, Max said, "No offense, but if you start barking questions at her, she's sure to be even more afraid than she already is."

"I choose to take offense," Wolfe retorted. "I'm not a cop, I don't depend on bright lights and rubber hoses to get answers. And if you believe I'd ever terrorize or knock a woman around, all I can say is you need a reality check. Aside from a personal aversion to that kind of thing, if Mother thought any of us had raised a hand against a woman, we'd be carrying our heads around in paper bags."

"That's a good point," Max admitted, his smile widening. "I take back the offensive remark. But I still think I should be the one to talk to her."

"Why? Because you've fallen for her?"

Max stared at him, then said, "Is it branded on me somewhere, or what?"

Grinning a little, Wolfe said, "Hey, if you think I haven't noticed you haunting the museum for no good reason, think again. Even if I wasn't here much myself, I recognized the signs days ago." Then he sobered. "If things are as bad with her as you seem to believe, I don't envy you. Especially if she's being pressured to help a thief get at your collection."

"I know. She's right on the edge. If I push too hard . . ."

"Yeah, but if *he* pushes too hard, the same thing's going to happen. We have to know for sure, Max. And soon. Even though the opening's still eight weeks away, and even though the collection won't be taken out of the vault until shortly before that, we can't afford to have a thief with eyes and ears inside the museum. Especially now while we're installing all the security."

"I don't think last night was a test of our security," Max said slowly. "I think it was a test of Dinah."

"To see if he could control her?" Wolfe nodded. "If you're right about her, that makes sense. It would explain why he did it so long before the exhibit's in place—so we wouldn't be unduly alarmed. It would also explain why he picked an entrance so far from anything of value and didn't even attempt to come in."

"That was my conclusion," Max said.

After a moment, Wolfe continued. "The simplest thing to do in order to protect both Dinah and your collection would be to remove her from the museum.

If she can't help the thief by being on the inside, the threats would likely stop."

"If it comes down to her safety, that's just what I intend to do. In the meantime, I have someone keeping an eye on her."

"Someone?"

Max said lightly, "A hired gun, you might say. Don't worry, he won't get in your way."

Wolfe was frowning slightly, and his eyes searched his brother's intently. "So . . . you're going to try to find out how Dinah's being threatened and by whom, while I sit on my hands?"

"While you continue to get the bugs out of the computer system and think up a few more cute tricks to protect the valuables," Max corrected.

After a moment, Wolfe nodded. "Okay. I'll play along for now, Max. But just so we understand each other—as long as Lloyd's holds the policy on your collection, I'll do whatever I have to do to protect it."

"I wouldn't have it any other way," Max said honestly.

When Max showed up in the doorway of her office just before noon and asked if she was ready to go to lunch, Dinah wondered if he was playing some kind of cat-and-mouse game with her. Nothing else made sense. He knew she had opened that door. He *knew* it. She'd seen it in his eyes this morning. Yet he hadn't said one word about it.

And in the museum it was business as usual, as if nothing threatening had occurred. The night guards had gone home, the day guards were in their accustomed positions, and visitors wandered through the halls and galleries. Ken Dugan had convinced himself the open door had merely been an accident and, after cautioning the employees to be more careful, appeared to have put the matter out of his mind.

Wolfe Nickerson had been around briefly during the morning, but he hadn't talked to anyone except Max and Ken, and had been gone now for over an hour. Dinah had been waiting for the other shoe to drop.

When she looked up and saw Max, she heard the thud.

"Are you ready?" he repeated, his tone pleasant. And before she could offer an excuse, he added, "There's something I need to talk to you about, and as soon as possible. It's still chilly out, you'll need your coat."

With her nerves already stretched to the breaking point, Dinah didn't have a hope of winning against his determination. There was even a part of her that wished he would get it over with and make the accusation, so she wouldn't have to keep waiting for it. She rose silently from her desk and got her coat, tensing when he came into the office to hold it for her but managing not to jump out of her skin.

Fifteen minutes later, with scarcely another word having been spoken between them, they were seated at a secluded table in a quiet restaurant a few blocks from the museum. When Dinah had shaken her head silently in answer to the waiter's query about before-lunch drinks, Max had ordered coffee for them both and the waiter left them alone with menus. There was a spectacular view of the bay through the window beside their table, and Dinah kept her attention in that direction.

"Dinah?"

"Yes?"

In a deliberate tone, he said, "Just so it won't be left hovering in the air between us, I'm pretty sure you opened that door last night. I believe you were forced to do it by someone who's threatening you."

Dinah turned her head with a jerk and stared at him in astonishment.

He nodded. "I need you to trust me. I want to find out who's doing this to you."

"I don't know what you're talking about," she said tonelessly.

"Dinah, listen to me." He leaned toward her, the expression in his eyes compassionate and his voice gentle. "I know you're afraid. I know this bastard has you convinced he can hurt you. But I'm not going to let that happen."

She wanted to believe him. She almost did. She'd forgotten what it felt like to be safe, to not be afraid, and the possibility that a haven was in reach was tempting. But Dinah had learned a hard lesson two years before. Safety was an illusion, and a horrifyingly frail one at that. Locks on the doors and windows, security devices, a police guard—nothing could keep a person safe if someone wanted badly enough to hurt her.

Admitting nothing, she said steadily, "If I'm under suspicion, it would probably be best that I resign from the museum." The caller had made threats about what he'd do to her if she took that easy way out, but what choice did she have? All she could do was run. Again.

Since their waiter returned with coffee then, Max couldn't respond until the man had left. As soon as they were alone again, he said, "No one wants your resignation, Dinah. I want to help you. Can't you believe that?"

She shrugged jerkily. "I had heard you were a philanthropist. But with your own collection at risk . . . no, I can't. And even if I could believe it, there's nothing you can do to help me."

"What makes you so sure?" he demanded.

Dinah looked at him with eyes that were too old for her lovely face, and replied softly, "Experience."

Max had intended that today would be only a beginning. A chance to convince her he wanted to help. It hadn't been in his mind to press for too many answers, because he didn't think she would confide in him easily. It would take time, that was only natural. But now, looking into those shadowed eyes, he knew he couldn't wait. He had a great deal of patience, but she was in pain and he couldn't bear that.

He couldn't even attempt to help her until he knew what had happened to cause her pain.

After a moment, he summoned their waiter and lunch was ordered. Dinah seemed to choose at random from the menu, and only picked at the food when it came. Max talked casually, asking no questions and saying nothing of any importance. He wanted to put her at ease, but knew that wouldn't happen. They had been strangers yesterday, and today he needed to know what secret caused her such awful fear. That meant he would have to break down the normal barriers between strangers as well as the one she had built around her secret.

He had no intention of making that attempt here. So he waited until the meal was finished—or, rather, until it became obvious Dinah wasn't going to eat anything more. When they left the restaurant, he put her into his car but, instead of driving back to the museum, he stopped at a small park about half a mile away. He would have preferred a more private location, but every instinct told him that even the suggestion of their being alone together would frighten Dinah.

"Why are we stopping here?" she asked nervously as he cut off the engine.

Max hesitated, then got out of the car and came around to her side. Opening her door, he said, "Our talk isn't finished, Dinah. Why don't we sit on that bench over there in the sunlight for a few minutes?"

"I have to get back to the museum," she protested.

"It's all right. I told Ken I might keep you out a little longer."

Dinah wanted to be angry, but she felt so damned

powerless. He made use of his own power without thought, possibly even without realization, to get what he wanted. He wasn't blatantly high-handed about it, but that hardly made the situation better from her point of view. The truth was, he could have her fired, arrested, almost anything, and she couldn't fight him.

She couldn't fight at all.

Ignoring the hand he offered, she got out of the car and walked the short distance to the bench he'd indicated. She sat down at one end, trying to think of a way out. Her hands were in the pockets of her coat not because it was chilly, but because they were shaking and she didn't want him to see that. She gazed off absently toward a group of preschoolers in the distance playing some game while their mothers watched.

Max sat down with only a few inches of space between them and half turned to look at her. Casually, he said, "You didn't tell me much about yourself last night, even though I asked. There's something I'm especially curious about, since you cut all your ties to come out here. Your family. Is there any particular reason why you and your brother aren't close?"

"Is this part of the talk?" she asked.

"Yes."

Get angry, she told herself. *It's the only way you'll be able to keep him away.* But it was difficult to be angry when all her energy was taken up by fear. If he hadn't been with her, she would have been looking constantly over her shoulder, jumping at every sound. As it was, she was abnormally sensitive to her surroundings. Every sight and sound was filtered through her fear and worry, examined and weighed carefully for a threat, and the tension was a constant drain on her strength.

She was so tired, she could barely think straight.

"No," she said finally, lying, not looking at him. "Sometimes siblings are just too different to be close.

That's the case with Glenn and me. We have . . .
nothing in common."

"And your parents?"

"They were killed when I was in college. A boating
accident."

"I'm sorry."

It took effort, but she managed to keep from
looking at him. "Are we finished now? May I get back
to work? Or do I go directly to jail?"

"Dinah, if I'd wanted you arrested, you'd be in jail
now." His voice was still quiet, calm, infinitely
patient—yet somehow relentless. "I only want the
truth. I want to know what happened to make you
discard your past. And I want to know who's threatening you now. Let me help you."

"What makes you think I've discarded my past?" It
was the first thing she could think to say, as panic
began to close up her throat. "People move across
country all the time, that doesn't mean they're running away from anything. Just because I came
here—"

"You come here to start over," Max insisted. "A
year ago, Dinah Layton didn't exist. Driver's license,
social security number, bank accounts, and credit
records—none of them more than ten months old.
You changed your last name, Dinah. You got rid of
your background, cut all ties to your past. And
people don't do that unless they *are* running away.
From something."

Her throat was tight, her eyes burning. She could
feel the tension inside her winding tighter and
tighter, and in the pockets of her coat her nails dug
into her palms painfully. With no one to confide in,
the fear, anguish, and horror locked within her had
no outlet at all, and the pressure was becoming
unbearable. She was afraid to move, certain the
slightest motion would shatter her into a million
pieces.

Couldn't he see that? Or had sheer practice made

her so adept at hiding what she felt that even now, when she was on the ragged edge of control, there was no outward sign?

"I'd like to leave now, please," she said in a thin voice.

"Dinah—" He reached to touch her shoulder.

She flinched violently, drawing into herself, and turned her head to stare at him with wide eyes.

Max froze, his fingertips barely half an inch away from her shoulder. Slowly, he drew his hand back, holding her gaze with all the will he could command. "Who hurt you, love?" he asked softly. "Who was he?"

She didn't hear the endearment. She didn't hear anything at all. Something had happened, something beyond her control. It was the strangest sensation, as tangible as a physical touch. A tugging at all her senses and emotions, as if he held one end of a line connected to her deepest self. She felt curiously protected, guarded . . . safe. Everything else seemed to retreat until it was too distant to be disturbing.

"Tell me," he said.

She had no choice. She had to tell him, just the way she had to go on breathing. "I don't know who he was—is. They never caught him," she murmured in a faraway tone. "Even though it's been nearly two years since—since it happened."

The chill inside Max spread and grew colder. He'd been afraid it was that, afraid she'd been hurt in the most vicious way a woman could be hurt. His chest ached, and he felt a rage at the thought of any man causing her such terrible anguish. He wanted to pull her into his arms and hold her, wipe away the pain and fear. But he didn't dare. Instead, very slowly, he lifted his hand again and touched her shoulder. He could feel her tense even with just that unthreatening contact, but her gaze was still fixed on his and she didn't draw away.

"He followed me here," she said. "The police said he wouldn't, that men like that don't . . . don't return to the same woman a second time. But I was so afraid he would, and they couldn't swear to me he wouldn't . . . or protect me if he did. When I couldn't stand the fear anymore, I left Boston. I moved all the way out here and started over. I didn't want to take any chances so I was careful. I changed my name. I changed everything. But it didn't do any good. He found me."

Max forced himself to speak calmly, even though it was hardly how he felt. "How do you know it was the same man, love?"

She blinked and looked vaguely puzzled for an instant, but her answer was unhesitating. "Because it's just like before. The phone calls first. A voice I'll never forget, so whispery and cruel. The . . . gifts. Wilted flowers, left outside my door during the night. Then, a few days ago, he—"

She blinked agian, this time holding back tears, and her voice shook uncontrollably. "I woke up, and he was there. On . . . on top of me in the bed. He had a knife. Like before. He said . . . he said he'd do it again, hurt me again, worse this time. Unless I did what he wanted."

The image she'd drawn in his mind made Max want to kill another human being for the first time in his life. And it made him angry at himself. A few days ago, before he'd had anyone watching over her, that was when the sick bastard had terrorized her. Damn, why hadn't he moved faster!

"I was so afraid," she whispered. "I—I couldn't think. The police couldn't stop him, I knew that. They didn't stop him before."

"Did they try?" Max asked gently.

"In Boston?" The tears she'd been holding back trickled down her ashen cheeks. "At first, when he began calling and leaving the—the gifts, they said they couldn't do anything, because he hadn't actually hurt me. But then another woman was raped by someone who had called and left gifts for her, and they thought the same man might be after me."

"What happened?"

"They set a trap," she whispered. "I agreed because I wanted them to catch him. Because I wanted to . . . to *do* something. And . . . they said they could protect me. There were police all around my apartment, and they had my phone tapped. But he never stayed on the line long enough for them to trace his call. And the days went by without a sign of him. When . . . when he finally did come after me, it was obvious he was just amused by what the police were trying to do."

She drew a shaky breath. "He . . . he got in without tripping the alarms. And he had a little box with him, like one of those machines that makes a soothing noise to help you sleep. He left the box for the police to find, as if he didn't care, as if he were taunting them. They said it made something called white noise. It blocked all the microphones and listening devices the police had put in my bedroom. So—so they couldn't hear what he was doing to me. They were right outside, just yards away, and they couldn't stop him because they . . . they didn't know he was there. They didn't know he was hurting me."

Dinah's eyes held an expression Max wished he had never seen—the pain of a wound so deep and still open even after nearly two years. The last thing he wanted to do was make her go through all this, but it was too late to stop.

"How long did you stay in Boston after that, Dinah?" he asked gently.

"I stayed for months," she answered tonelessly, as if all feeling had been squeezed out of her. "Everyone—all the doctors and counselors—told me it would get better. They said I'd heal and stop being so afraid. My friends said so too. And my brother,

Glenn. But I never felt safe, no matter how many locks were on the doors and windows. And the fear kept growing. Finally, I knew I had to get away from Boston. I knew I had to start over."

"So you came here?"

She nodded. "A friend at the trauma center told me how I could change everything—my name and the records. I had a little money from my parents' estate, enough to move out here and get settled. Enough to let me get by until I could find a job. The curator of the museum where I worked in Boston wrote a wonderful reference for me, and he was understanding enough to be willing to use my new last name. So I was pretty sure I could get a good job.

"The rest was simple. I moved out here last fall. I found a part-time job, and kept it while I looked for something better. When I got the job at the museum last week . . . I thought I was really going to be able to start over."

"But then he called?"

Dinah shivered violently. "He called."

Max felt even more reluctant to go on with this, but he had to find out everything and he hoped it would be better for her to get it all out at once. "Dinah, are you sure it was the same man?"

"He whispered." Her answer was nearly inaudible. "I'll never forget that voice. As soon as I heard it, I knew it was him, that he'd found me. At first, I thought it was another nightmare, but . . . it was real."

Max wanted to pull her into his arms, hold her. He wanted to promise her she was safe now, that he'd take care of her. But after what had happened with the promises of the police two years ago, he knew she wouldn't believe him. The rapist had done more than hurt and terrorize her—he had shattered her trust, her ability to feel safe, and her faith in promises.

"I wanted to run again," she said unsteadily,

"but . . . but he said he'd only find me. And kill me. I believed him. So I did what he wanted. I opened the door last night. And I went into the exhibit's wing, to see where the nearest entrance was. I'm sorry. I'm sorry, but I didn't know what else to do."

"It's all right, Dinah. I don't blame you. No one will blame you." He put every ounce of reassurance he could muster into his words, and held her shoulder very gently.

"I didn't want to do it," she murmured. "But I was so afraid. So afraid . . ."

"I know. Don't worry about it anymore. I won't let him hurt you again, love, I promise." The vow slipped out before he could stop it, driven by his intense need to reassure her that he could protect her. But, just as he'd expected, Dinah simply didn't believe the promise.

"You can't stop him. The police tried to stop him, they had lots of men and equipment—"

"Never mind the police." She was exhausted, he could see that, and what she needed most of all was rest. She was still gazing at him as if she couldn't look away, and he took advantage of that fragile connection. Softly, he said, "I need you to trust me, Dinah. You're very tired, and you need to rest. I can't take you back to your apartment, because you won't be able to sleep there. You haven't slept much in days, have you?"

She shook her head. "No. Because he might get in." In those simple words were echoes of stark terror.

"I want to take you somewhere he can't get in. To a place where you'll be safe, where you can rest. Will you let me do that?"

"Where?"

"My apartment." He felt her stiffen. "It's all right, love, I promise. My housekeeper's there, and she'll stay with you. I only want to make sure you sleep for a while. Will you let me do that? Will you trust me?"

.

Trust him? She thought she did, but she couldn't seem to reason clearly at the moment. Nothing in her head made much sense, all she was sure of was the weariness dragging at her. She felt herself nodding slowly in answer to his gentle question, and didn't protest when he rose from the bench and drew her up as well. She allowed him to put her into the car, and sat silently beside him when he got in.

He was right, she needed sleep. Maybe when she woke up, she'd find that all this was just a dream, a nightmare. She heard his voice, realizing he had called someone from the car phone, but she didn't listen to the words. He asked her gently what her name had been before she'd changed it, and she told him it had been Lockwood.

Or maybe that was only in her mind. The possibility of all this being a nightmare made her frown, and she struggled to understand why that likelihood didn't seem pleasant.

Oh. Him, of course. Max. If all this were no more than a dream, then obviously she'd dreamed him too. It made sense that he was part of the dream. Wouldn't any woman in her position dream such a dream? As in the childhood fairy tales she remembered, a prince appeared to save the poor, cursed princess, and they lived happily ever after.

Except that dreams ended when sleep did.

Dinah's foggy mind refused to allow any more thought. She was vaguely aware of the car stopping, of Max helping her out. There was a building and the sense of space, then the movement of an elevator. Max kept talking to her, but she didn't listen to the words, only to their soothing sound. After a while, there was another voice, a woman's voice, kind and motherly. Max stopped speaking, but the nice woman went on talking to her gently. Someone helped her undress and put her into a soft, warm bed.

She felt safe, and it was such a relief that she

completely let go for the first time in a very long time. The nice woman's voice faded away, and the shaded room became the silent darkness of total peace. She slept so deeply, she didn't even dream.

Eventually, the blackness seemed to lessen, and she did have a dream. At least, she thought it was a dream.

She dreamed that she got out of bed and made her way across a dim and unfamiliar room to the door, because voices had awakened her. She opened the door only a couple of inches, but instantly the voices reached her clearly, and she could see a light down the short hallway that must have been coming from a den or living room. There were two voices. One was Max's. The other, also male, was unfamiliar to her, unrecognizable.

". . . and that's all there is to it," Max said in a rough tone that didn't invite argument.

"I didn't suggest anything else. Calm down, Max," the other man said quietly. "Obviously, you're not about to use Dinah to reel this guy in. I understand that, and I agree. All I'm saying is that he went to too much trouble finding someone inside to give up just because you've cut his string. He wants the collection, and he'll try again."

Max's response sounded distant for a moment, and then clearer, as if he was moving around the room restlessly. "You agree with me, though? He isn't the bastard who hurt Dinah two years ago?"

"I'd say not. Rapists don't usually become thieves, according to all I've heard."

"I want both of them," Max said with chilling mildness. "That animal two years ago, and the sick bastard who's terrorizing her now. I want them both roasting in hell."

After a slight pause that felt very tense to Dinah, the other man said reasonably, "Max, we might— stress might—be able to get the guy here, but the one in Boston? You read the police reports, there wasn't even enough evidence to find a single suspect. He was damned sophisticated. He knew they had her staked out, but he came after her anyway—*with* some state-of-the-art electronics of his own to neutralize their bugs."

The visitor sighed audibly. "He thumbed his nose at them, but he wasn't careless. He didn't leave tracks. And there hasn't been another attack matching the M.O. since what happened to Dinah—at least not one that was reported to the police. If the bastard didn't get run over by a bus, then all we can assume is that he's either changed his M.O. or he's stopped. Either way, he's out of reach."

"You sound like a cop."

"Perish the thought. And, hey, don't shoot the messenger, all right? I'm just pointing out what you already know yourself. Unless he surfaces in a very public way, that animal in Boston is out of your reach."

"I can't accept that," Max said.

"You have to. Besides, think of Dinah. She'll never feel safe if you go digging around in what happened two years ago. Let it lie. Our best bet is to concentrate on what's been happening here."

Max was silent for a long moment, then sighed audibly. "All right, you've made your point. So . . . how do we get him without using Dinah to do it?"

"Like I said, he wants the collection. He'll try something else. We'll just have to be ready for him."

"Am I right in thinking he isn't the one you're after?" Max asked.

The other man sounded a bit wry. "Unfortunately, yes. My target works solo, he never uses an accomplice or a tool. Was it you or me who said thieves would be coming out of the woodwork once you decided to exhibit the collection?"

"I don't remember, but it seems to have been prophetic."

"I'll say." The stranger sighed. "I'm sorry, Max. I

didn't realize it would get so damned complicated. There's still time to cancel the exhibit, if you'd rather."

"No, I'm in for the duration. Just do what you can to put a name or a face to this bastard, all right? And we'll weed out at least one of the thieves."

"You mean *you* will."

Three

Dinah didn't recollect much more of the dream, except for closing the door again and returning to bed. When she finally woke, sunlight streamed through the draperies and her internal clock told her she'd slept for a long, long time.

She sat up slowly and looked around, unable to figure out for a moment where she was. This wasn't her room, her bed. She was in a lovely old four-poster bed, which was only one of the gleaming antiques in the bedroom. The draperies and bed-spread were a floral design, with pastel colors, and she had the sense this was a woman's room rather than a man's. She looked down at herself, baffled and a little unnerved to see she was wearing a simple but beautiful silk nightgown.

It wasn't hers, any more than the room was hers.

Then the last tendrils of fog drifted out of her mind, and she remembered. Max. She had told him all of it; somehow, he had pulled the truth out of her. She was in his apartment, and had been since just after they'd had lunch. But how long had that been?

"Well, good morning."

Dinah looked around quickly, the voice touching a chord of familiarity in her. The woman standing in the doorway was middle-aged and plump, her graying hair neat and her face kind. For the life of her, Dinah couldn't recall if any introduction had been made.

"Morning?" she ventured hesitantly. Surely it wasn't Saturday morning?

"It's nearly eight o'clock."

It was Saturday morning. For heaven's sake, she'd slept more than fifteen hours!

The woman smiled. "I'm Mrs. Perry, Mr. Max's housekeeper. You probably don't remember much of yesterday. Are you feeling better?"

"Yes, thank you." Dinah glanced back down at the nightgown, and added, "Just—a little puzzled. Have I been asleep since yesterday afternoon?"

"You needed the rest, if you don't mind my saying so." Briskly, Mrs. Perry added, "The bathroom's right over there if you'd like to shower before breakfast. Your clothes are on that chair, cleaned and pressed. Mr. Max has one of his business calls right now, but he'll join you for breakfast. It should be ready in about half an hour."

Feeling distinctly overwhelmed, Dinah murmured, "Thank you." Then, as the housekeeper began to turn away, she said, "Mrs. Perry? What about this?" She fingered the silk nightgown.

Understanding all the shades of meaning in the question as any other woman would, Mrs. Perry smiled. "I helped you into that yesterday. It belongs to Mr. Max's mother. She's a delicate thing, like you. Still beautiful, and still has men bending over backward to please her. He keeps this room ready for her, since she passes through San Francisco several times a year."

Which, Dinah thought as the door closed quietly behind the housekeeper, answered most of her questions about the nightgown. But as she slipped from the comfortable bed and went to shower, all the other questions crowded into her mind.

Max had been amazingly kind, and she didn't know why. Had he called her love? More than once? Surely not, that didn't make sense. He'd spoken to her for the first time only two days ago! He'd said something in her office yesterday about love at first sight—but he hadn't meant himself. Had he? Men like Max Bannister didn't fall in love with strange women who hid their past and helped criminals. The very idea was ridiculous.

She was imagining things. That had to be it. He was just a kind man. Exceptionally kind. He'd felt sorry for her, and he'd brought her back here to get some rest.

Having reached that logical and reasonable conclusion, she felt unaccountably depressed. She got out of the shower and dried off, then got dressed. She found a brush to untangle her damp hair, and a new toothbrush obviously left for her.

When she was finished in the bathroom, she put her shoes on and ventured out into the hall. She was a little wary, but much more her normal self than she'd been in days. She looked around curiously, counting three bedrooms aside from the one she'd used, and emerged from the hallway into a huge and beautiful sunken den complete with floor-to-ceiling windows with a spectacular view of the bay and a marble fireplace. Antique furniture was mixed with contemporary pieces, creating a perfect blend of quiet good taste and comfort.

An archway led to a dining room, the massive oak table set for breakfast for two, and another doorway in that room led, presumably, to the kitchen. There was a set of double doors beyond the fireplace, one of which was open about a foot, and Dinah could hear the murmur of Max's voice.

She slid her hands into the pockets of her slacks and moved slowly in that direction with no idea of what she could—or would—say to him.

". . . since I approved the plans months ago, I

don't see why you need me now," Max was saying as she stepped into the room. He was half-sitting on the corner of an intricately carved oak desk, the phone to his ear and his gaze turned toward another splendid view of the bay through the windows in this room.

Dinah didn't listen to what he was saying, but looked around the room. A workingman's home office, not just for show, she realized. The books on tall shelves bore the multicolored dust jackets of books purchased to be read rather than the embossed leather bindings of expensive "libraries" intended to impress others. Near the desk were two oak filing cabinets and the latest thing in computer work stations, with the computer screen alive with scrolling lines of neatly grouped words and figures. A drafting table was set up next to the windows. There was also a long leather couch grouped with several matching chairs, and a low, wide coffee table that held a jumble of magazines and newspapers.

"Do your best, David. If I have to, I'll fly out next week. All right."

Dinah looked back at Max just as he hung up the phone, and she still didn't know what she was going to say to him. He looked different, casual in a sweater and jeans rather than the suits she'd seen him wear. He seemed subtly more powerful, more . . . masculine. That she was so aware of him, so conscious of his physical presence startled her. And when he turned his head and saw her, when she met the instant warmth in his gray eyes, she felt the most peculiar little leap of her heart.

"Good morning," he said, straightening and smiling at her.

"Good morning." A part of her wanted to look away, but she couldn't. "This is taking philanthropy a little far, isn't it?"

"You've thought it through, and that's the only answer you can come up with?" he said lightly.

"Something like that."

"Do you need coffee in the morning?"

Dinah stared at him. "Yes."

"Then let's go have breakfast." He came toward her, still smiling. "Maybe after coffee and a meal, you'll be able to think of something better."

She allowed herself to be guided from the room, increasingly baffled. The rest had left her calmer and less apt to jump out of her skin, but with a clearer mind she couldn't help wondering if his motives were neither philanthropic nor romantic, but simply practical. After all, if someone was trying to use her to get to his collection, he'd naturally want to find out who that was. . . .

The dream came back hazily, and as she took her place at the table she tried to remember more clearly. Max, talking to another man whose voice she hadn't recognized. Max saying implacably that he wouldn't use her to get to the thief, that he wanted the thief and the animal in Boston roasting in hell. . . .

What if it hadn't been a dream?

She watched as he filled her coffee cup from a silver pot, her mind suddenly still and cold. *Two of them?* As horrible as it was to believe a rapist had followed her for two years and across three thousand miles, it was somehow worse to consider that a ruthless thief had learned of her pain and terror and had used both to his advantage.

"Dinah?"

She looked at him and forced herself to ask the question. "Is the man here . . . the one from Boston?"

Max, seeming to realize how difficult it was for her to ask, replied quietly, "It's unlikely. Rape is an act of violence, with no motive except sickness. Men like that don't suddenly turn to large-scale theft—or not rape again when they have a victim at their mercy."

Dinah had always flinched from any talk of what had happened to her, and most people who had known about it avoided mentioning it. That attitude had only worsened her inevitable feelings of shame and guilt, and allowed no outlet for her anger. Even her brother . . . She brushed the memory away hastily, unwilling to recall that other pain.

Max was different. He didn't look at her with speculation as if wondering what she'd done to get herself raped. His sympathy and compassion weren't uneasy or forced, and there was an odd look of pain and muted anger in his eyes, as if what had happened to her had somehow hurt him as well.

To say she felt comfortable talking about it would have been a considerable overstatement, but she found herself able to talk about it—and it was the first time she'd felt that way.

"Then the man here was acting a part? He wouldn't have hurt me?"

Max hesitated. "I believe he was acting a part, but I can't say he wouldn't have hurt you. If he is after the collection . . . It's priceless, Dinah, people have been killed for a lot less. Even if he isn't the one from Boston, any man cruel enough to do what he did to you is capable of anything."

"Then, if I hadn't done what he wanted—?"

"He might have followed through on his threats. If he believed you were his only hope, there isn't much doubt he would have been even more ruthless. From his actions, it's clear he thinks of you as a means to an end, that's all. A tool to help him get what he wants."

"But . . . why me? And how did he find out about . . . about Boston?"

Max studied her for a moment as if judging her state of mind, then answered matter-of-factly. "My guess is that he'd already checked the backgrounds of the other museum employees, and couldn't find a handle anywhere. No possibility of controlling any of them with fear or blackmail. Then you were hired, so he checked your background and ran into a wall.

People discard their pasts only for a reason, and he went looking for yours. It isn't too difficult to track someone if you have at least one fact—he knew you'd worked for a museum in Boston. The reference is on file at the employment office, remember, and he obviously had access to those records."

She drew a breath and let it out slowly, accepting that Max was probably right. "He did everything just the same way. Even how he spoke . . ."

Max reached over and covered one of her hands with his, gripping it firmly. "Dinah, every one of the facts was in newspaper articles and police reports. Everything, even the fact that the Boston rapist whispered. A male voice whispering is virtually unidentifiable even though it may sound distinct, and he obviously knew that. It's the whisper you remembered, not the voice."

It made sense, but Dinah was still confused. "The police reports? He could get those?"

"It's possible, even likely. All he needed was a computer and a few contacts to get the information. After we came back here yesterday, I was able to get all the information within a couple of hours."

His hand was heavy and warm, and she didn't try to pull away. "You? You know . . . all of it?"

"I didn't want to invade your privacy," he said, explaining his motives. "But I felt I needed to know whatever the thief knew about you, and I didn't want to have to question you anymore. Do you understand?"

Dinah half nodded, then looked away and gently pulled her hand from under his as Mrs. Perry came into the room. The housekeeper was quick and efficient, setting their plates before them and telling them cheerfully to let her know if they needed more coffee, then left them alone again. Dinah didn't usually eat breakfast, and her appetite lately hadn't been strong at all, but she found herself hungry now.

Max didn't press her to talk, waiting until the meal was finished before he said anything of importance. Then, pouring fresh coffee for both of them, he asked, "Have you thought of anything better?"

For a moment she didn't know what he meant, but then she remembered his earlier guess as to what she'd been thinking. The question of his motives. She sipped her coffee to give herself time to think, but it didn't help. "No," she said finally. "Unless . . . you need me to catch the thief."

"No way," he said instantly with a touch of the implacability she remembered hearing in what she'd thought was a dream. "I'm not about to let that bastard terrorize you again, or give him even a chance to hurt you more than he already has." He hesitated, then added in a milder tone, "In fact, I want you to stay here until we get our hands on him."

It was the last thing she'd expected. "What?"

Max went on talking reasonably as if she didn't look stunned. "You should be safe at the museum during the day, and I'll take a few precautions just to be sure. I'm there most days anyway, so getting you there and back won't be a problem. And the security in this building is the best in the city—aside from which this apartment has a system the world of larceny doesn't even know about yet. You'll be safe here."

"No," she said.

"Of course you will."

Dinah shook herself out of the stupor. "That's not what I meant, and you know it! I can't stay here."

"Why not?" He was smiling just a little.

She opened her mouth, closed it, and then said a bit desperately, "I hardly know you."

"If you're worried about the proprieties, Mrs. Perry is going to stay here at night." His light tone changed when he added, "If you're worried about me, please don't. I would never do anything to hurt you or frighten you, Dinah."

She had a curious feeling of being trapped as she gazed into his steady gray eyes, and realized with a shock that she was on the verge of agreeing with his plan. Hastily, she pushed back her chair and rose, going out into the den as she silently tried to shore up her resistance. Was the man a warlock?

"Dinah." He had followed her, not giving up. He was, after all, Maxim Bannister, and he was accustomed to getting what he wanted.

She swung around to face him, one hand resting on the back of the couch as if she needed support. She thought she might, especially since he was no more than a couple of steps away. "I can't move in here with you for the duration." Before he could speak, she added quickly, "I heard— I thought it was a dream, but I heard you and some other man talking last night. Didn't I?"

He frowned slightly. "You could have. Why?"

"Because he said the only way you'll be able to get the thief is to wait for him to make another move. That could take weeks, even months if he waits until the exhibit's been open for a while. I can't stay here that long."

"Why not?"

"Stop asking me that! You know why not. Look, I—I'm grateful for what you did yesterday, bringing me here and letting me rest, but I'm not your responsibility."

"Dinah, you'll never feel safe in your apartment again, we both know that."

Just the thought of returning to her apartment made a shiver of dread crawl up her spine. The man here in San Francisco might not be the one from Boston and he might not be a rapist, but she was afraid of him and of what he could do to her. "That isn't your problem," she managed.

"Yes, it is. I made it my problem." He took half a

step closer to her. "Can't you just accept my help for the time being?"

"No." She shook her head, fighting him as well as a cowardly urge to give in. "He's been watching me, I know it; he must know you brought me here. He'll think you found out, that I'll be no use to him now because you know what he's trying to do. He won't follow me when I . . .when I leave San Francisco, especially if it's the collection he wants."

"So you'll run again?" Max asked quietly.

Dinah felt a wave of shame, but lifted her chin. "You don't know what it's like," she said unsteadily.

"No, I don't know," he agreed. "I can't even imagine what it feels like to be hurt and terrorized the way you've been. But I can see the effects of it in your eyes, and I don't have to feel it myself to understand what you've been through. I do understand. I know you want to get away from the sick bastard here as badly as you wanted to escape the one in Boston, and I know running seems like the only way out— but it isn't, Dinah. If you run now, you'll never stop."

She leaned against the back of the couch and crossed her arms over her breasts, feeling cold. "Maybe. But at least then I'll have some kind of control, even if it's only the decision of where to go next."

"You'll never feel safe."

"I'll survive."

"As what? As a woman who allowed a greedy, soulless bastard to destroy her life a second time?"

At his harsh words, Dinah could feel herself wavering, stung again by a sense of shame and a reluctance to see herself as a coward. She couldn't protest or deny his words, couldn't defend herself. The truth was that she was afraid.

Dinah was not, by nature, a timid woman. Her experience of violence and brutality had changed her, but the underlying strength she possessed had enabled her to take what positive steps she could to reclaim the life a rapist had stolen from her. She had almost succeeded, too, conquering the fear to the point that she'd been able to sleep nights and had stopped looking back over her shoulder.

But then it had happened to her again, and the traumatic shock of being forced to relive that terrible time in her life had been literally paralyzing. Her terror had been even greater this time, because she had *known*, without a doubt, all the horrible ways he could hurt her. Her memory had tormented her far more than imagination ever could have. And after the inability of the police to protect her the first time, she had felt utterly and completely alone and vulnerable. Powerless to do anything at all to help or defend herself.

But now, after Max's soft accusation, she realized that it could well destroy her to run a second time. To uproot herself and cut her few fragile ties to this place, to allow herself to be driven away. She would never recover, never heal from what had been done to her, if she didn't fight in any way she could to take back her life.

Knowing that, however, was easier than accepting it. And easier than accepting the help of a virtual stranger when her trust in others had been shattered so completely.

Max slid his hands into his pockets and stood gazing at her, his eyes filled with disturbing emotions she couldn't read. Then, softly, he said, "If you won't stay for yourself, stay for me."

"I told you—you aren't responsible for me."

He shook his head slightly, holding her gaze. "That isn't it. My motives are almost entirely selfish. I want you here with me. I want to see you every day, talk to you, listen to you. I want to prove to you that you can trust me." He smiled crookedly. "I can't do any of that if you run away."

Dinah wasn't sure which she believed—that his interest in her was as personal as he'd made it sound, or that he'd found a masterly way to manipulate her. She didn't ask, because she didn't know him well enough to recognize when he was lying. Yesterday he had persuaded her to talk, to trust him, but she wasn't exhausted anymore and she couldn't afford to trust him now.

People you trusted could hurt you so terribly.

Dinah wasn't willing to risk that, not when so much else was beyond her control. But even as she began to shake her head, Max lifted a hand to stop her.

"Wait. Hear me out."

He was too persuasive, and a part of her didn't want to listen to him—but part of her did. After a slight hesitation, she shrugged. "I guess I owe you that much."

"Give me two weeks, Dinah."

She frowned. "To do what?"

"To find a way of catching this bastard. It's a reasonable request, isn't it? You said it might take months, and that you couldn't stay here indefinitely. Give me two weeks to try to catch him. Stay here for that long and give me a chance to try."

She was still frowning. "You mean, I might be able to help?"

Max began to shake his head, then stopped. "I don't know, maybe something you remember could help. That's always possible. But it isn't why I want you to stay. You need to give yourself time, find out if there are other options. You've started over here, don't let him ruin that. Give me two weeks to try to remove the threat."

Dinah didn't see what he expected to happen in two weeks. Logic said the thief would lie low for a while and consider his own options. He had plenty of time to contemplate another way of getting to the collection, after all, since it wouldn't even be in the museum for two months. But it was a reasonable request, and she couldn't help wondering if Max, even though he'd denied it, believed she *could* help in some way. If that was so, she did owe him the chance to find out, if only because he had been unusually kind and understanding.

And because it was a step in the right direction. A step toward getting control of her life. If she could take some part in helping to capture the man who had terrorized her, it could only help her.

Max must have seen or sensed her wavering, because his voice became even more persuasive. "Two weeks, that's all. You'll be safe here and at the museum, you won't have to look over your shoulder all the time, and if we're able to catch him, you won't have to run."

"You're very determined, aren't you?" she murmured.

Max smiled. "Very. I won't force you to stay here, but I'll do my level best to talk you into it."

Dinah had burned her bridges once before, and some maniac had found a way into her past despite that. This time, she felt a growing need to stay and fight in whatever way she could—if she could. And though she didn't want to admit it even to herself, her greatest regret in leaving San Francisco would be turning away from Max.

She didn't know him, wouldn't let herself trust him, and had her doubts about his motives, but there was something in his eyes that affected her in a way she couldn't even put a name to, something that pulled at her. She owed herself the chance to find out what it meant.

Finally, she nodded. "All right. I'll stay for two weeks. But at a hotel—"

"No, here. He could get to you in a hotel, he won't get to you here."

"Once he knows I talked to you, that I stayed here last night, he probably won't even try," she protested.

"I won't risk your life on a *probably*," Max said softly.

The protest had been made out of a sense of what was right, and nervousness about being in Max's home, but Dinah was glad to be overruled. One thing she was certain of was that she didn't want to stay alone. The man after her here might not be the same one from Boston—and a part of her was still unsure of that, still unwilling to totally believe it—but he was dangerous, and she was afraid of him.

"All right. Here." She hesitated a beat, then added, "Thank you."

Max was smiling again, and sounded a little hopeful when he said, "Do you think you could learn to say my name without prompting?"

She couldn't help smiling back. "I'll see what I can do about that . . . Max."

"Thank you. Now why don't I take you back to your apartment so you can pack, and we'll get you settled in here?"

Late Monday afternoon, Dinah looked up when she heard a light knock on the open door of her office, and smiled without thinking when she saw Max.

"Ready to go?" he asked.

"I need about ten more minutes," she replied, indicating the paperwork she'd nearly completed.

"Okay. I should try to catch Morgan before she leaves anyway, so I'll meet you in the lobby."

Dinah nodded and, after he'd gone, used five minutes of her allotted ten in thinking about the past few days. It was odd, but even though she knew safety was an illusion, she felt safe with Max. And completely comfortable in his home.

He had helped make the transition amazingly easy with his casual attitude and undemanding companionship. By Sunday, he'd even been making her laugh. Aside from an occasional business call, he had spent most of his time with her and had focused his entire attention on her without making her overly conscious of it, or causing her any discomfort at all.

He had put her completely at ease in his presence, and she wasn't even sure how he'd done it. She had found herself talking about her likes and dislikes to him, gleefully beating him at poker, and sharing one rather heated political discussion. On Sunday morning they'd taken over the kitchen to make French toast, with Mrs. Perry a pained observer, and lunch became a picnic in the Golden Gate park.

It was only now, thinking back that Dinah realized just how swiftly and completely he had put her at ease. Even now, he had made her feel closer to the woman she had been before the rape, as if the pain and fear of the past two years were lifting away from her, loosening its grip. She had returned to work today with more confidence than she'd felt in a long time, and hadn't been terribly surprised when no one asked her awkward questions about where she had been since lunchtime on Friday.

Max wouldn't have liked that.

The people around him gave Max their total loyalty, almost as though by instinct. Yet it wasn't something he asked for or demanded. It was something he earned. He treated people with respect, fairness, and an unusual degree of empathic understanding. He truly seemed able to feel what others felt even though he might lack their painful or disagreeable experiences.

It was a rare trait, and an endearing one. How could anyone resist a man who, when he said, "I understand," really *meant* the words? How could anyone avoid standing a bit straighter in his presence, and feeling both stronger and better only because he saw something in you that you hadn't known was there?

Almost against her will, Dinah was beginning to

trust him. To believe his promises. She told herself it was only because she wanted to believe, because she had accepted his help and was terrified of being disappointed yet again by broken promises and worthless "protection."

But it was more than that. She had the odd notion that he was helping to heal her not by surrounding her with safe walls, but simply by loaning her some of his strength until she was strong enough to stand on her own. And in that way, he helped to heal her pride as well as her wounds. It was a part of his unique charisma, his ability to affect those around him in ways as subtle as they were positive.

Dinah was beginning to realize that Max's strength and his beneficial effect on others came less from who he was than what he was—and discovering just what he was had become a fascinating experience.

She returned to her unfinished work, a shade of uneasiness creeping into her mind. They hadn't talked at all about the thief who was after Max's collection, but they'd have to, she knew. If he wasn't caught . . .

Out in the lobby, Max was listening to Morgan explain why one of the newly built display cases for the exhibit wasn't going to work.

"So we have to go back to the drawing board," she finished, sounding exasperated. "Damn, you'd think at least *one* of us would have realized the thing wasn't going to fit. And now they say redesigning that case might affect the two closest to it."

"Are we going to lose time on this?" Max asked.

"No way. If anyone even suggests we push the opening back, I'll have his head," Morgan replied firmly.

Chuckling, Max said, "Then I'll leave the matter in your capable hands." He saw her glance at her watch, and added, "Have a date?"

"For my sins, yes." She grimaced slightly, then

laughed a little. "He seems to be a creature of the mind, but we'll see."

Meditatively, her boss said, "I've always found that the mind can go only so far in controlling the instincts."

"Well, if he can't control *his,* he'll earn a right-cross. Honestly, Max, if I tangle with one more lusting beast hiding behind a puppy-dog smile, I'm going to join a nunnery."

"Keep your chin up," Max advised, smiling. "Somewhere out there has to be one man who'll value your brain as much as your body—and you'll probably fall over him while you're looking for something else."

"If you say so." Morgan sighed. "Anyway, I'd better go. Tell Dinah I'll see her tomorrow."

He nodded, and stood alone in the lobby, brooding as he waited for Dinah to join him. *The mind can go only so far in controlling the instincts. . . .* He was learning the truth of that. His mind told him Dinah needed more time, but his instincts were in revolt. He had wanted her from the moment he'd first set eyes on her, and nothing that had happened since had changed that.

She wasn't afraid of him now, and he was reasonably sure she was at least beginning to trust him, but he didn't know what would happen when he told her how he felt. He didn't know if he could help heal what had been done to her, or if any move on his part would send her running away from him. For one of the few times in his life he was unsure, his instincts telling him the time was now and his mind insisting he should wait.

All he needed was a sign from Dinah, even the barest hint of a feeling that was more than friendship or gratitude, but he'd seen no sign at all from her. She seemed to regard him as a rather enjoyable companion; he wondered if he even saw him as a man.

Reluctant to put that question to the test, Max reined his instincts and continued to wait. The casual atmosphere between them remained unchanged as they returned to his apartment and enjoyed a quiet evening together. Max had a couple of calls to make after dinner, and Dinah curled up on the couch with a book borrowed from his office.

It was late when he came out into the den. Mrs. Perry had gone to her room, and the fire in the marble fireplace had burned down to a few flickering flames. In that soft, wavering light, Dinah slept peacefully on the couch.

Max stood gazing down at her for a long time. Her vibrant hair shimmered, red burnished by sparks of gold so that the silky strands had a life of their own. The dark crescents of her lashes lay against the flawless cream of her complexion in a vivid contrast. And her lips, slightly parted, were beautifully shaped, softly red, beckoning Max so irresistibly he could actually feel their physical pull.

He wanted to join her on the couch, to kiss her awake and hold her in his arms. To make love to her until she had no memory of violence, or pain, or any man except him.

The only thing that stopped him, the only reason he was able to control the fierce need he felt for her, was his certain knowledge of just how fragile trust could be. This woman had been terribly hurt at the hands of a man, her entire life shattered almost beyond repair, and that she could even begin to trust another man was something of a miracle.

Max wasn't about to jeopardize that.

After seeing the depth of her fear and knowing what had caused it, watching her sleep with trust and serenity in his home more than made up for his own increasingly restless nights. Still, as he sat down carefully on the edge of the couch beside her, he had to hope, had to believe there was a special bond between them. Nothing else could explain how quickly she had become comfortable with him.

She had fallen asleep with the book lying open over her stomach, and as he eased it away from her, her gleaming eyes opened drowsily.

"Hi," he said softly, laying the book aside on the coffee table and smiling at her.

"Did I fall asleep?" she murmured.

"Yes. I hated to disturb you, but if you spend the night out here you'll have a stiff neck in the morning."

"What time is it?"

"Almost eleven."

Dinah began to sit up, and Max caught her shoulders to help her. Since he didn't move away, they ended up physically closer than they'd ever been before.

Dinah was simply startled at first, but that reaction lasted no longer than the space of a heartbeat. What she felt then shocked her so much, she couldn't move. Staring into his gray eyes, she felt a strange, growing warmth inside her, and all her senses came vividly alive. It was as if a part of her that had been sleeping for a long time was now awakening.

He lifted one hand from her shoulder and brushed a strand of coppery hair off her face, his fingers lingering to stroke her cheek. "Have I told you you're beautiful?" he asked in a voice she'd never heard from him before. It was low and deep as always, but there was an intensity now, a suggestion of strong emotions held in check by an iron fist.

"No." She couldn't look away, and her skin seemed to tingle and glow beneath his touch.

"You are. I thought so the first time I saw you."

"Max . . ." She didn't know what she wanted to say, the words wouldn't come. Something about this happening too fast perhaps, or disbelief that it was happening at all. Her thoughts were tangled, her emotions confused.

"It's all right, Dinah. I know you aren't ready for anything more, not now." His voice was gentle, but the note of leashed desire remained. "But one day you will be, I hope. And I intend to be here. Haven't you realized yet? It's why I couldn't let you run away."

Her eyes widened as he leaned closer, then drifted shut when his mouth touched hers. He kissed her with a gentleness that made her throat ache, without demand and yet without concealing his own powerful need. It was a very brief touch, but she felt changed by it, marked somewhere near her soul.

The words still wouldn't come to Dinah. Surprise, uneasiness, wonder, bafflement, and the response of her senses to him all churned inside her. But the strongest emotion was the pang of disappointment when he drew away, and that shocked her a great deal.

How could she feel this way?

Max got to his feet and held her hands to help her up, then stood looking at her for a moment before he spoke. "It's late, and you wanted to get to the museum early tomorrow. You'd better turn in. Sleep well."

Dinah hesitated, then shook her head a bit helplessly and moved away from him. "Good night," she murmured.

"Good night, Dinah."

He watched her until she disappeared into the hallway, fighting the urge to call after her, follow her, something. To stay where he was and say nothing when he wanted so badly to be with her tonight—and every other night—was one of the hardest things he'd ever had to do in his life. That he was able to remain still and silent was due only to his growing hopes. He was making progress, he knew it. She hadn't stiffened or drawn away, and he had felt her tentative response to the brief kiss. For now, it was enough.

Max didn't know, then, that an unexpected meeting on the other side of the city was about to set a series of events in motion—events that would have a profound impact on a number of lives, and ultimately determine the fate of the Bannister collection.

Four

Morgan West's measurements had been causing her problems since her thirteenth birthday. She couldn't find fault with her height—which, at five feet five, was about average—and she rather enjoyed having black hair and skin that tanned easily, both courtesy of a Cherokee ancestor who had also tossed high cheekbones, a certain amount of ferocity, and pride into the genetic pool.

But the amber eyes bequeathed by the Irish branches of her mother's family tree were, Morgan thought, too large and looked ridiculous fringed by long, thick, curling, ink-black lashes that nine out of ten people automatically assumed were false. At sixteen, she had tearfully demanded that her family doctor thin them out, but he'd refused. The years had reconciled her. She never had to wear mascara, which any woman would consider a definite plus, and there were worse things than having to say "Yes, they're real," fairly often.

Unfortunately, she had never reached a point of acceptance regarding her figure.

There were men who admitted that long, shapely female legs inspired amorous fantasies; there were those who had the same basic response to the rich curves of swaying hips. But men whose primitive instincts were aroused by an ample bust, Morgan had found, undoubtedly outnumbered the others.

And hers was certainly generous. Her dates during high school and college had been so entranced by her "charms," she often wondered if they knew what her face looked like. Even the Rhodes scholar she'd briefly gone out with—hoping his mind was on a higher plane—had stuttered dreadfully whenever his gaze had strayed to her chest. Which was often.

A fortunate combination of genes had also bestowed on her a tiny waist, which many men were compelled to span with their hands in delight, making her feel absurdly like Scarlett O'Hara, gently curved hips, and a firm backside, which—according to eagerly expressed opinions—looked great in jeans. At thirteen, Morgan had been both pleased and flustered by the attention; at eighteen, however, she'd begun to feel more than a little grim.

The situation hadn't improved in the years since. Morgan might have taken pride in her centerfold proportions, except that the Creator had seen fit to be equally generous with her brain. (Sitting atop a body that had on more than one occasion quite literally stopped traffic, and nestled behind big eyes with all the guardedness of a startled kitten, was an excellent mind.) In fact, Morgan's tested and retested I.Q. put her comfortably in the minor-genius range.

People without extraordinary beauty or extraordinary dimensions sneered at the statement that it can be a curse; still others insisted that the cover of a book must always match its contents; and to most a forty-two-inch bust indicated an I.Q. of approximately the same number.

Morgan had heard it all. She had been treated—by men and women alike—as if she were an ornament, a sex kitten, or an idiot. Or all three. Through bleak experience, she'd discovered that proving herself as an intelligent woman was a constant, ongoing struggle.

Which was one reason Maxim Bannister had won her intense and total loyalty. He had, to be sure, gulped visibly when she'd first walked into his office, but he had also conducted the hour-long interview without allowing his gaze to stray to her chest—and without making her feel it required all his concentration to avoid staring. And since that time, he had managed not only to make her feel completely comfortable in his presence but had even responded with genuine sympathy when a particularly degrading experience with a date had caused her to unburden herself in an explosion of temper.

She liked Max a lot. He was one of the very few male friends she'd ever had, and she was delighted by the knowledge that, while he was no less appreciative of nature's bounty than the next man, his awareness and interest were not driven by hormones. He also had an unerring eye for color and style, and during the months of preparation for the Mysteries Past exhibit, she had gradually abandoned her dark-colored, loose blouses and multilayered outfits in favor of more elegant and flattering clothing.

When Max told her she looked good in something, she knew it was the truth. He'd said once that she was a queenly woman, the observation made in an assessing rather than complimentary tone, and Morgan had, quite unconsciously, begun walking without the slump she had just as unconsciously adopted in her teens.

She hadn't realized for a long time what was happening. Then she had noticed that Max brought out the best in people because he *saw* it there. A word at the right moment, a sincere compliment, strengths and weaknesses pinpointed so the former could be encouraged and the latter either avoided or gently improved. People *bloomed* around Max.

It was the most fascinating thing Morgan had ever seen, and when she looked in a mirror she was astonished. In a few short months, he had very quietly, gently, and unobtrusively eradicated both Morgan's bitterness and the chip on her shoulder. Thanks to him, she was as proud of her body as she was of her mind.

Well, nearly.

Which wasn't to say it no longer caused her problems. In fact, masculine appreciation of her measurements was, she supposed, indirectly to blame for a predicament that was destined to occupy her for quite some time.

She had buried herself in work in recent years, but after Max's healing wizardry Morgan began, somewhat tentatively, dating again. It was just bad luck, she told herself, that the young curator who had always treated her with grave respect turned out to have a baser motive lurking under his smiles.

He was perfectly charming during dinner, and then afterward asked if she'd like to go to his museum and see the latest Egyptian exhibit, which wasn't scheduled to go on display for several days. It wasn't exactly "Come up and see my etchings," but since she'd recognized the look that went along with the casual offer it was enough to make her wary.

Still, she wanted to see the exhibit. The hours she put in overseeing her own forthcoming exhibit would make a visit during regular hours somewhat of a problem, but she was confident of her ability to handle an amorous curator. There would be security guards, in any case.

"That's funny," her date murmured as he used his key and let them in a side door.

"What?"

"The security light in this hall should be—"

It should have been on, Morgan knew, but her escort never got a chance to finish his sentence. They had taken no more than three steps into the dark hallway when he suddenly let out a soft grunt and crumpled to the floor.

Afterward Morgan was never sure if she *knew* what had happened in that first instant or if, in the thick blackness surrounding her, pure survival instinct had taken over. She didn't reason that Peter's limp body had fallen between her and the door, blocking that exit, she simply whirled and bolted down the hallway.

After half a dozen steps she managed to kick her heels off without losing much speed, and her instantly quieter passage made it possible for her to hear the pursuing footsteps—fast and heavy, and all too close behind. She had the advantage of knowing the museum well. Like many archaeologists, she considered the storehouses of ancient treasures as alternate homes, and tended to spend many of her off hours losing herself in the past.

That was what she wanted badly to do now—lose herself in the past. She was making her way with all the speed she could muster out of the warren of offices and storerooms and into the larger rooms of the museum proper. There was a drawback to that action, but she had little choice. Most of the exhibits were individually lighted, which would make her visible to her pursuer unless she could hide before he emerged from the hallway. As she turned the final corner, she could see the dim glow ahead.

The first cavernous room she burst out into was a hall of paintings offering no place of concealment. Barely feeling the cold, hard marble beneath her feet, Morgan darted through one of the two big archways without immediately knowing why she'd made the choice. Then she realized. There had to be more than one intruder in the museum and they'd be after the most portable valuables, wouldn't they? That could only be jewelry, and a large display of precious gems lay in the direction she hadn't chosen.

Along her route were several larger and, to the thieves, less valuable displays of statuary, weapons, and assorted artifacts, many large enough to offer a hiding place.

She made another desperate turn through an archway that appeared to house a room dimmer than some of the others, and found herself neatly caught. A long arm that seemed made of iron rather than flesh lifted her literally off her feet, clamping her arms to her sides, and hauled her back against a body that had all the softness of granite. Then a big, dark hand covered her mouth before she could do more than gasp.

For one terrified instant, Morgan had the eerie thought that one of the towering statues of fierce warriors from the past had reached out and grabbed her. But when a low voice hissed in her ear, the impression of supernatural doings faded.

"Shhhh!"

He wasn't a security guard. The hand over her mouth was encased in a thin, supple black glove, and what she could see of his arm was also covered with black. Several hard objects in the vicinity of his waist dug into her back painfully. Then he pulled her impossibly closer as running footsteps approached, and she distinctly felt the roughness of wool—a ski mask?—as his hard jaw brushed against her temple.

Better the devil you know than the one you don't . . . The thought ran through her mind, but for some reason she didn't struggle in the man's powerful embrace—probably because she didn't know the devil out in the hallway any better than she knew this one. Instead, she concentrated on controlling her ragged breathing so that it wouldn't be audible, her eyes fixed on the archway of the room. She realized only then that she'd bolted into a room with only one entrance. Her captor had literally carried her into a shadowy corner behind one of the fierce warrior statues, and she doubted they were visible from the doorway.

The footsteps in the hall slowed abruptly, and she caught a glimpse of a rather menacing face further distorted by an angry scowl as her pursuer looked into the room. She stiffened, but he went on without pausing more than briefly. As the footsteps faded, she began to struggle. The steely arm around her tightened with an additional strength that nearly cracked her ribs.

Three breathless seconds later, she realized why.

"Ed." The voice, low and harsh, was no more than a few feet down the hallway.

Morgan went very still.

There was an indistinguishable murmur of at least two voices out there, and then the first voice became audible—and quite definitely angry.

"I thought she came this way. Dammit, she could be anywhere in this mausoleum—the place is huge!"

"Did she get a look at you?" Ed's voice was calmer.

"No, the hall was too dark. When I tapped her boyfriend to sleep, she ran like a rabbit. Why the hell did he have to pick tonight to come here? If he wanted romance, he should have taken her to his place. Judging by what I saw of her, she'd have kept him busy between the sheets for a week."

Stiffening again, this time with indignation, Morgan was conscious of an absurd embarrassment that the man holding her so tightly against him had heard that lewd comment.

"Never mind," Ed said impatiently. "We're covering all the doors, so she can't get out, and the phone lines have been cut. Go back to your post and wait. We'll be finished in another half hour, and out of here. She'll be locked in until morning, so she can't do us any harm."

"I don't like it, Ed."

"You don't have to like it. And stop using my name, you fool. Get back to your post."

There was a moment of taut silence, and then Ed's unhappy minion passed the archway on his route back to his post, an even fiercer scowl darkening his face.

Morgan heard his footsteps fade into silence. Strain as she might, she couldn't hear anything from Ed. At least five minutes must have passed, with agonizing slowness, before her captor finally relaxed his grip on her and eased her down so that her feet touched the cold floor. His voice sounded again, soft and no more than a sibilant whisper, next to her ear.

"I'm not going to hurt you. Understand? But you have to be still and quiet, or you'll bring them down on us."

Morgan nodded her understanding. As soon as he released her, she took half a step away and turned to confront him. "If you aren't with them, what are you—" she began in a whisper, then broke off as she saw the answer to her question.

He was a tall man, an inch or two over six feet, with wide shoulders and a wiry slenderness about the rest of him that spoke of honed strength rather than muscled bulk. She'd felt that strength. Enveloped in black from head to foot, he had a compact and very efficient-looking tool belt strapped to his lean waist. And from the black ski mask gleamed the greenest pair of eyes she'd ever seen.

"Oh." She knew, then, what he was doing here. "Oh, God."

"Not nearly," he murmured.

Morgan felt a burst of pure irritation at his ill-timed humor, but somehow managed to keep her voice low. "You're just another *thief.*"

"Please." He sounded injured. "Such a commonplace word. An ugly word, even. I prefer to call myself a privateer."

"Wrong," she snapped. "This isn't a ship on the high sea, and we aren't at war. You're a common, ordinary, run-of-the-mill *criminal.*" She could have sworn those vivid green eyes sparkled with sheer amusement.

"My dear young woman," he said, "I am neither common nor ordinary. In fact, I'm one of the last of a vanishing breed in these uncomfortably organized, high-tech days. If you must attach a noun to me, make it 'cat burglar.' However, I'd much rather you simply called me Quinn."

Morgan stared at him. Quinn? Quinn. She knew of him. Lord, of course she knew of him! For nearly ten years, the name of Quinn—along with assorted aliases and journalistic nicknames in various languages—had been synonymous with daring, nerveless theft at its most dramatic. If the newspapers were to be believed, he had smoothly robbed the best families of Europe, relieving them of fine baubles and artworks with a delicate precision and finicky taste that made the "cat" in his preferred noun an apt choice. And in so doing he had bypassed some of the most expensive and complicated security systems ever designed with almost laughable ease. Also according to the newspapers, he never used weapons, had never injured anyone, and had never come close to being caught—all of which made him something of a folk hero.

"Hell," Morgan said.

"Not yet." He seemed even more amused. "I see that my reputation preceeds me. How gratifying. It's nice to know that one's work is appreciated."

She ignored the levity. "I thought you were a European thief exclusively."

"Ah, but America is the land of opportunity," he intoned in a reverent voice.

She didn't know whether to laugh or swear again. It disturbed her to realize that she—be it ever so reluctantly—found him amusing. With her own love of ancient artifacts and priceless artworks, she had never felt the slightest urge to romanticize the theft of them. And no matter how rapturously certain journalists described the daring exploits of thieves with taste and without any leaning toward violence, she saw nothing of a Robin Hood-type myth clinging to this one: No one had ever implied that Quinn shared his spoils with the poor.

"What are you doing here?" she demanded.

"I rather thought that was obvious."

Morgan drew a deep breath. "Dammit, I meant— Stop staring at my chest!"

Quinn cleared his throat with an odd little sound, and in a suspiciously pensive and humble tone, said, "I have held in my hands some of the finest artworks the world has ever known. Had I but realized a few moments ago that so exquisite a work of Nature herself was so near . . . May I say—?"

"No, you may not," she said from between gritted teeth, fighting a mad urge to giggle. It cost her something to stop him, because the words were certainly lovely enough if one cared for that sort of base flattery—not that she was impressed by them, of course.

"No, naturally not," he murmured, then added sadly, "there are certain drawbacks to being a gentleman burglar."

"Oh, now you claim to be a gentleman?"

"What's your name?" he asked, ignoring her question.

"Morgan West." Oddly enough, she didn't even think about withholding the information.

"Morgan. An unusual name. Derived from Morgana, I believe, Old Welsh—" This time, he stopped himself, adding after a thoughtful moment, "And familiar. Ah, now I remember. You're the director of the forthcoming Mysteries Past exhibit."

She raised a hand and shook a finger under his nose. "If you *dare* to rob my exhibit," she said fiercely, "I will hunt you to the ends of the earth and roast your gentleman's carcass over perdition's flame!"

"I believe you would," he said mildly. "Interpol itself never threatened me with more resolution."

"Never doubt it." She let her hand fall, then said in an irritable tone, "And you distracted me."

"Not nearly as much as you distracted me, Morgana."

"It's Morgan. Just Morgan."

"I prefer Morgana."

"It isn't your name—" She got hold of herself. Absurd. Of all the ridiculous . . . Here she was in a dark museum that was being looted by an organized group of thieves; her dinner date had been, at the very least, knocked unconscious; she'd been chased through marble halls by a man who probably wouldn't have been nice if he'd caught her; and now she was defending her name preference to an internationally famous cat burglar who had too much charm for his own good.

And hers.

Doggedly, she tried again. "Never mind my name. If you aren't with those jokers out there, then why are you here?"

"The situation does have its farcical points," he said amiably. "I'm afraid I dropped in on them. Literally. We seem to have had the same agenda in mind for tonight. Though my plans were, of course, on a lesser scale. Since they outnumber me ten to one, and since they are definitely armed, I chose not to—shall we say—force the issue. It breaks my heart, mind you, because I'm almost certain that what I came here for is now neatly tucked away in one of their boring little leather satchels. But . . . *c'est la vie.*"

Morgan stared at him. "What did you come for?"

"None of your business, Morgana," he replied quite gently.

After a moment, she said, "I don't suppose you'd let me see your face?"

"That wouldn't be my first choice, no. Quinn is a

name and a shadow, nothing more. I have a strong feeling that your descriptive powers are better than the average, and I don't care to see a reasonable facsimile of my face plastered across the newspapers. Being a cat burglar is the very devil once the police know what you look like."

He had been leaning a shoulder against the stone warrior, his pose one of lazy attention, but before she could reply to his statement, he straightened abruptly. She didn't have to see his face to feel his sudden tension, and when he reached out for her she felt a moment of real fear.

"Shhhh," he whispered, drawing her close to him and deeper into the shadows. "They're coming."

The man must have ears like a bat. She hadn't heard a thing, but was now aware of the muffled footsteps coming toward them up the hall. A lot of muffled footsteps.

Quinn bent his head until his lips were near her ear and softly breathed, "Their truck's parked by a side entrance. They have to pass this room in order to reach it."

Morgan was definitely nervous about the possibility of discovery, but even then she was aware of a totally extraneous and illogical observation. Despite Quinn's implication that if he had known about her charms earlier he might have allowed his hands to wander a bit, the hand at her waist remained perfectly still and had not "accidentally" fumbled en route there. It was to his eternal credit as a man, she thought. Or a credit to his detached professionalism as a thief with more businesslike matters on his mind. Or else he had been grossly exaggerating his admiration of said charms. She wasn't sure which.

She wanted to know, though. She very badly wanted to know.

Pushing the insanely inappropriate thoughts aside, she tried to ignore the disturbing closeness of his hard body as they watched almost a dozen shadowy forms file quietly past the doorway. All the men carried leather satchels and were burdened with various tools. Morgan watched them, and it suddenly hit her that the small brown bags contained the museum's treasures.

The realization was like a kick in the stomach; it hurt and made her feel ill. She couldn't just stand here and watch without lifting a finger to stop them—

But Quinn quickly and silently clapped his hand over her mouth again, and the hand at her waist held her in an iron grip that defied her to attempt any movement.

She felt very peculiar. How had he known? Surely the wretched man couldn't read minds? No. No, of course not. She must have given away her feelings somehow. Twitched or whimpered or something. She made herself stand perfectly still until he finally relaxed and turned her loose about ten minutes later.

"My ribs," she said, "are cracked. At least three of them."

"Sometimes I don't know my own strength," he apologized solemnly.

She followed as he strolled casually out of their hiding place and into the hall, reasoning from his lazy attitude—and the fact that his deep voice was no longer unnaturally quiet—that he knew the other thieves had gone. "What happened to the security guards?" she asked.

"It's just a guess," he answered, walking through the hall with more briskness now, "but from the way they were snoring when I checked on them earlier, I'd say they'd been drugged. And nicely trussed as well. You heard the charming Ed say that the phone lines had been cut. The alarm system has naturally been deactivated, and none of the outside doors were damaged when they came in—Damn." The oath, uttered with more resignation than heat, escaped him as they stood in the doorway of what had been the Egyptian exhibit.

Morgan said something a great deal stronger. In fact, she said several violent and colorful things, the last few of which caused Quinn to turn his head and look down at her.

"Such language," he reproved.

"Look at what they *did!*" she very nearly wailed, gesturing wildly at the room as the echoes of her bitter cry bounced mockingly back at her. It looked, she thought painfully, like a room after a child's party: Messy, depressingly empty, and rather pathetic.

The thieves had been thorough. Into their little brown satchels had gone all the literally priceless jewelry of the pharaoh and everything else they could carry away. Figurines, the gold plates and goblets meant to hold the food and drink of divine royalty in the afterlife, even—

"The mummy case," she gasped. "They took it too?"

"Carted it out before you crashed the party," Quinn answered, still maddeningly calm.

Morgan turned and seized fistfuls of his black turtleneck sweater, rather pleased when he flinched visibly as her nails dug into his chest. "And you didn't even try to stop them?" she demanded furiously.

"Ten to one," he reminded in an absent tone. "And they had guns. Don't hit me, but you look rather magnificent when you're angry."

She snarled at him and gave him a shove as she stepped back. The shove didn't budge him, which also, and in an odd way, pleased her. "You are a soulless man," she told him. "How anybody— anybody at all—could stand here and look at this . . . this *rape* in total calm passes the bounds of all understanding."

"Appearances," he said softly, "can be quite deceiving, Morgana. If I could get my hands on the man who ordered this done, I would probably strangle him." Then, in a lighter and rather mocking tone, he added, "Such wholesale thievery has a distressing tendency to enrage the local constabulary, to say nothing of persons with valuables to protect. And it's so greedy, aside from the trouble it causes us honest craftsmen."

"Honest?" she yelped.

"I have my living to make, after all," he said in an injured tone. "Can I help it if my natural skills set me in opposition to certain narrow-minded rules?"

She looked blankly after him as he turned away, then scurried along behind him. The floor was cold under her stockinged feet, and it reminded her . . . "Oh, Lord, I hope they haven't killed Peter," she muttered almost to herself as she caught up with Quinn.

"The boyfriend?"

"My date," she corrected. "He's the curator of this place."

"And he brought you here after hours? Let me guess. He wanted to show you his etchings?"

Morgan didn't have to see his face to know it would have looked sardonic. His tone told her as much. But his question was so damned apt that she had a difficult time being indignant.

Finally, sweetly, she said, "None of your business."

"That's put me in my place," he murmured, then before she could explode, added, "I wouldn't worry about your Lothario. Professional thieves tend to avoid murder."

"Does that go for you too?" she asked nastily.

He was unruffled. "Certainly. The judges of the world, by and large, look on robbery with severe eyes—but not nearly so severe as those regarding murder."

Morgan couldn't manage anything but a sneer, which was wasted because Quinn was rapidly surveying the rooms they were passing through. Interested despite herself, she asked warily, "Are you looking for something?"

"I hate wasted efforts," he explained absently.

She almost tripped over a security guard lying on the floor, his hands taped behind his back and—as Quinn had said—snoring gustily. Regaining her balance, she hurried on, catching up to the infamous thief as he stood looking down into a glass case.

"The Kellerman dagger," he said thoughtfully.

She didn't like his tone. "What about it?"

"It's a nice piece. Gold haft studded with rubies. Plain sheath, but what the hell. Fetch a good price."

"What?" Morgan was so enraged, her voice actually squeaked. "You don't think I'm going to just stand here and let you steal that?"

"No." He sighed. "No, I rather thought you'd have an objection." And then he moved.

Afterward, Morgan was unable to explain to her own satisfaction how he managed to do it. He didn't exactly leap at her, he was just *there*, in a flash like a big shadow. She was off balance. That was her only excuse. Off balance and lulled by the sinful charm of the thieving scoundrel.

She found herself, quite unaccountably, sitting on the cold marble floor. She wasn't hurt at all. Both her wrists were bound—snugly but not too tightly— together with black electrician's tape, and she was staring at the ornate leg of the display case, which her arms were wrapped around. Effectively immobilized.

She tried to kick him, but he was too agile for her.

Chuckling as he stood just out of her range and removed something from his tool belt, Quinn said admiringly, "Your eyes spit rage, just like a cat's. No, stop trying to kick me, you'll only hurt yourself."

Morgan winced as the glass in the display case shattered under his expert touch. "You're not going to leave me here?" she demanded incredulously, peering up at him.

"Sorry," he murmured.

"You—you bastard!"

He might have heard the note of genuine horror in her voice; his head tilted as he looked down at her, and his low voice was more sober. "Only for an hour or so, Morgana, I give you my word. As soon as I'm away, I'll tip the police."

She scowled at him, angry at herself for having shown a moment of weakness. The truth was, she did not at all enjoy the idea of being alone, helplessly bound, in a dim museum with only drugged guards and a possibly murdered Peter for company. She hadn't realized it until now, but Quinn's insouciant manner and easy strength had been—in some peculiar way she didn't want to think about—more than a little comforting. Even if he *was* a devious, rotten, no-good criminal.

"Is your word any good?" she asked coldly.

He seemed to go very still for a moment, then said, "My word is the only good thing about me. One must, after all, cling to some scrap of honor."

The overly light tone couldn't quite disguise a much deeper feeling underneath. Morgan couldn't hold on to her scowl, but she managed not to soften toward him. Much. She watched him lift the dagger from the case and drop it into a chamois bag she hadn't noticed tied to his tool belt. Then a sudden memory made her say, "Ed said I'd be locked in until morning. How're you going to get out?"

"The same way I got in," he answered carelessly.

"Which is?"

His eyes gleamed, catlike, as he looked down at her. "Which is my little secret. After all I may use the same trick to get at your exhibit."

Her softening vanished as if an arctic wind had frozen it. "I swear to God, Quinn, if you lay so much as a single finger on any part of Bannister's collection . . ."

"I know," he said sympathetically when her choked voice trailed off. "It's so hard to rise to glorious heights a second time. The first threat was so marvelously phrased. Let's see—ah, yes. If I tamper with Mysteries Past, you mean to hunt me to the ends of the earth and roast my gentleman's carcass over perdition's flame. That was it, I believe."

She made a strangled sound of sheer rage.

He chuckled. "I must go now, *cherie*. Are you quite comfortable?"

Pride told her to ignore the mockingly solicitous question; the coldness of the hard floor beneath her thin skirt told her to speak up before he disappeared. Common sense won out, but her Cherokee pride made her voice sulky. "No, dammit. The floor's hard. And cold."

"My apologies," he said gravely. "I will try to remedy that." He vanished into the shadows toward another of the rooms.

Morgan had to fight a craven impulse to cry out his name. Museums were unnerving places at night, so *quiet*, with big, dark things looming in shadows, and the faint, musty smell of age and inexorable decay. She shivered, seeing the remnants of history from a new perspective and not liking it much.

Quinn returned in just a few minutes, carrying a tasseled pillow he'd gotten God knew where. Still sulky but curious, she waited to see how he'd manage. Her position on the floor was awkward and she couldn't raise herself. He stepped around behind her, bent, and slid one arm around her waist—again, with no exploratory fumbles. Then he lifted her a few inches and neatly slid the pillow underneath her.

"How's that?" he asked.

She looked up at him as he came into sight again. "Better," she said grudgingly. "But the police are not going to believe a ruthless thief took the time and trouble to put a pillow under my bottom."

He laughed with genuine amusement. "They will believe it. Trust me. Just tell them you asked for the pillow." The laughter fading, he stood looking down at her for a moment. "And tell them I was here. Don't forget that."

Morgan had the sudden realization that her story was going to sound awfully improbable. She found herself mentally editing Quinn out of the story completely, and was so astonished at herself she could only stare up at him bemusedly. "I—I don't—That is, I haven't decided what I'll tell the police."

He was silent for a few beats, then said softly, "Will you lie for me, sweet Morgana?"

"No," she snapped. "For me. In case you haven't realized, any story I tell is going to sound fishy as hell. Running from a group of organized thieves and caught by an internationally famous cat burglar who just happened to be burgling the same museum on the same night? After which, said thief tied me to the leg of a display case and put a pillow under my bottom before stealing a lone dagger and making good his escape? Don't forget that Peter and I got in with a key. What's to stop the police from suspecting I was in league with . . . with you or the other ones?"

"If you know how to play dumb," Quinn said dryly, "the idea will never cross their minds."

"I'll play hysterical," she snarled. "God, the messes I get into. Just because Peter had to show me his etchings. Stop laughing, you monster! Go on—get out of here, why don't you? Fade away into the misty night. Fold up your tent and beat it. Hit the road. The next time I see a black ski mask, I'll kick it in the shin. I hope the next place you burgle has a pack of wild dogs in it. Dobermans. *Big* Dobermans. Big *hungry* Dobermans—who missed their breakfast, lunch, and dinner."

She eyed him resentfully as he leaned against the display case.

"On the whole," Quinn said, "I think I'd prefer the flame of perdition."

"You can count on that. If Interpol doesn't get you, I will."

A last chuckle escaped him as Quinn straightened. "I find myself almost looking forward to that. Good night, sweet, and thank you for enlivening a boring evening."

She held out until he reached a distant, shadowy doorway, then said, "Quinn?"

He hesitated, then turned. She caught the flash of his green eyes.

"You—you will call the police?"

"I give you my word, Morgana," he said. "They'll be here within an hour."

She nodded, and in a moment the shadows were only shadows. It was very quiet, and curiously desolate. She sat there, bound to the leg of a display case, her stockinged feet growing cold—why hadn't she asked Quinn to find her shoes?—and a thick pillow cushioning her against the hard floor.

It occurred to her that she should start weaving a reasonable story for the police.

Knit one, purl two. No, that wasn't weaving. Weaving was Penelope picking out the threads of her tapestry by night because she didn't want to marry anyone else even if Ulysses *had* been gone an awfully long time. What were the odds against running into an infamous cat burglar twice in one lifetime? Remote. Unless, of course, one were the director of a fabulously valuable exhibit. . . .

"Well, officer," she said aloud in the cavernous room, "it happened like this . . ."

By the luminous hands of her watch, the police arrived forty-five minutes later. And Quinn had been right, damn him. They took one look at her and accepted without a blink the notion that a busy thief would take the time to find her a pillow because she'd said her bottom was cold.

There were benefits to looking like a dumb sex kitten.

Sometimes.

Once in a blue moon.

Five

"I don't like it," Wolfe said, slouching in his chair as he stared at a police report lying before him. "That makes two museums robbed within two weeks—and both on a grand scale. It sounds as if there's a very greedy gang in town, and I doubt they'll stop now."

The meeting could best be described as a brainstorming session, and was taking place very early in the day at a makeshift conference table in one corner of a cavernous storage room. With office space at a premium, it was the best way for all of them to be together comfortably, and had the added advantage of no ringing telephones or other interruptions. Max, Wolfe, and Morgan were present, as well as Dinah; Ken was at the burgled museum helping to take stock of what was missing.

After a moment, Max said, "Neither of those museums have the kind of security being installed here. Their systems aren't even as good as the existing system here. They relied on guards and simple door alarms. No lasers or sensors, and no backup system in case of electrical failure."

Wolfe shook his head. "That isn't what's bothering me. I'll grant the museums' security was outdated. What I don't like is the *scale*. That gang of thieves came in like an army, Max, and stole everything they could carry. According to Morgan, they were unhurried, methodical, and very businesslike. They didn't leave a fingerprint or a clue, and I can't see they made a single mistake. All we have is what Morgan saw and heard: Ten to twelve men, one of them named Ed, who very efficiently stole items no self-respecting fence would touch. That points to a major collector, or a cartel of them, being supplied by these thieves. And *that* means nothing stolen is likely to surface again. The police haven't got a hope in hell of finding that stuff."

"The dagger might surface," Morgan murmured.

Dinah, watching her, thought that the other woman seemed uncomfortable, but didn't say anything.

"What dagger?" Max asked.

Morgan cleared her throat and met his eyes. "The Kellerman dagger. The thieves—the group of thieves—didn't get that. Someone else did."

"Who?" Wolfe asked.

"Quinn."

Wolfe sat up with a jerk, staring at her. "Quinn? He was there last night?"

Nodding briefly, still looking at Max, Morgan said, "He was there. I didn't tell the police because . . . well, because if it hadn't been for him, that gang would have caught me and probably wouldn't have been nice about it."

"I thought they did catch you," Wolfe said slowly.

"No. They knew I was there, and they weren't very happy about it, but they didn't seem too worried either. It was after they'd gone that I was tied up. Quinn did that. I—uh—made a fuss when he decided to steal the dagger, so he tied me to the display case."

"Did you see his face?" Max asked.

"No, he was wearing a ski mask. He wouldn't tell me what he'd come there to steal originally. He just said that when he discovered he wasn't the only thief in the building—and was outnumbered—he decided to stay out of their way."

Max looked at her steadily for a moment, then said, "You seem to have had quite a conversation with him."

Morgan flushed a little, but continued to meet his gaze. "I can't really explain, except that I didn't feel threatened by him. I mean, I wasn't afraid of him at all. He was even sort of charming—and *don't* remind me he's no better than the others. I know that, believe me. It's just that if I'd told the police, it would have only complicated things and, besides, it sounded so improbable. It doesn't make a difference, does it? The only item he took was the dagger, and if he fences that it's bound to surface, so . . ."

Dinah spoke up then for the first time, a bit tentatively. "But if the dagger *does* surface, won't that lead the police astray? I mean, it could indicate to them that all the other items could be fenced as well, so they'd concentrate on the wrong assumption. Wouldn't they?"

"Common thieves versus collectors?" Max nodded. "It's likely, but I doubt Morgan's story about Quinn would have made much difference. Wolfe?"

The other man, frowning, looked up with a slight start. "The police? They have to follow standard procedure in robbery cases, which means they'll keep an eye on known fences. Not really much else they can do without a solid suspect. If the dagger surfaces alone, they'll try to follow that lead as a matter of course, but they won't go off track for long." He paused for an instant, then added, "If Morgan had blown the whistle about Quinn being there, it probably wouldn't have made a difference in the way the police work the case. If Quinn's in this country, the police'll know about it soon enough."

Dinah knew of Quinn, as most everyone involved with valuables did, but she knew little about him. "Is Quinn his real name?" she asked curiously.

"I doubt it," Morgan replied dryly. "In fact, I seem to remember an enthusiastic journalist in England using the name first because it means wise and intelligent, or something like that." She looked at Max, hesitated, then said evenly, "There haven't been any reported robberies by Quinn in the States until now. He came here, Max, straight here, to San Francisco. And he knew I was the director of your exhibit. I don't know what he was doing at the other museum last night, but I think the Bannister collection is his ultimate target."

"Great," Wolfe said a bit grimly. "Just how many thieves do we have to trip over before—and after—Mysteries Past opens to the public?"

Max was silent for a long moment, looking at each of the others in turn. "It isn't a totally unexpected problem," he said finally. "In fact, I think we all knew it was likely to happen. I certainly did. But it doesn't change anything. All we can do is make it as difficult as possible for any thief, or group of thieves, to get to the exhibit."

"I don't suppose you'd consider canceling," Wolfe said. It was more a statement than question.

"No. That isn't an option."

Morgan bit her lip, and said, "We could push the opening back a few weeks or months. Delay. The collection isn't in danger until it's in the museum or in transit. If we delay, maybe the police—"

"No," Max said again, "I don't think so. The police haven't a lead on that gang, they've *never* had a lead on Quinn, and if a collector or group of them is behind either, a delay won't make any difference." He shrugged. "All we can do is make security as tough as possible and keep our eyes open."

Wolfe stared at him, then rose without a word and left.

"Is he mad?" Morgan asked, lifting a brow at Max.

Max smiled slightly. "Of course not. He loves a challenge."

Chuckling, she gathered her copies of police reports and various notes, and got up. "Well, I'm getting on the horn to the security company right now. If their bright boys and girls know any tricks we *haven't* planned for security here, I want to know what they are. If we have to, we'll turn this place into Fort Knox."

Dinah waited until the other woman had left, then said, "Was he mad?"

"Annoyed, let's say," Max replied, still smiling. "I'm not making his job any easier. The most rational and logical thing to do would be to postpone the exhibit indefinitely and give the police time to make some headway with these robberies."

"Then why don't you?" she asked slowly, watching him. They were sitting on the same side of the scarred old wooden table, but almost facing each other.

"I made a promise. I said the collection would be exhibited to the public this summer."

"You always keep your promises?"

"Always."

Dinah was beginning to believe that.

Since Morgan had called before breakfast with news of last night's robbery and her own involvement, Max and Dinah hadn't had the chance to talk about anything else. In particular, they hadn't mentioned the turning point their own relationship had taken last night, and Dinah was feeling both a little shy and more than a little nervous about that. So she struggled to keep the conversation away from a subject she was wary of dealing with.

"It's odd the way Morgan met Quinn," she said.

"Do you really think so, or are you just nervous about being alone with me?"

It wasn't the first time Max had done that to her—picked up on emotions or motivations she'd much rather have avoided facing—but this time she didn't feel startled or uneasy. This time, she felt a bit irritated.

"It was a legitimate comment," she answered carefully.

"Of course it was. It was also whistling in the dark." He was watching her intently.

She had to agree that she'd made the remark more to keep the conversation away from them than out of driving interest. Her instincts urged her to avoid confrontation or conflict of any kind, but that two-year-old characteristic seemed to her, not for the first time, both cowardly and dishonest.

"Dinah?" he said gently.

She drew a breath. "You're wasting your time. I don't want a . . . a relationship. I can't feel what you want me to."

"Are you sure of that?"

"Yes."

"You aren't even willing to give it a chance?"

Dinah stared fixedly down at the sheaf of papers in front of her, fighting the almost overpowering urge to look at him. She wanted to say there was no chance, and why make an attempt that was doomed to failure, but she couldn't say anything at all. The truth was, a small, nervous part of her *did* want to try, even though the idea scared her. She had never known anyone like Max, and all her instincts told her there could be something special—maybe even enduring—between them.

But there was no chance at all unless she was willing to try, and even though she felt much more in control these days and no longer paralyzed by fear, she wasn't at all certain she was ready for that.

"Dinah? You gave me two weeks to try to find the man threatening you. Can't you wait at least that long before making up your mind about us?"

She felt fragmented, pulled in different directions. But some of the strain immediately eased when she found herself nodding. "All right." She sneaked a glance at him and, as always, was caught, unable to look away. "I don't mean to . . . dither so much," she murmured. "It's just that I'm afraid."

"I know," he said.

"I hate it. It's cowardly."

Max got to his feet and took her hands, drawing her up gently. "Dinah, if you weren't afraid, you'd have no sense and no imagination. It's perfectly natural to be afraid after what you've gone through." He smiled slightly, his eyes intent. "But you aren't afraid of me. Are you?"

"No." It was an instinctive answer.

"Good." His hands tightened around hers. "You've trusted me so far, I hope you'll learn to trust me completely."

"I don't know if I'm capable of that," she admitted. "Or ever will be."

Max released one of her hands so that he could touch her face. His fingers were warm against her skin, and when he cupped her cheek tenderly a pulse of pleasure throbbed through her body.

"You're capable of it," he murmured. He lowered his head, very slowly, until his lips touched hers.

Just as it had been the night before, Dinah felt sensations she had never known were possible, especially for her. A tingling blanket of warmth spread outward through her, and all her senses seemed to come alive. She could feel his hand slide beneath her hair, his fingers moving against the sensitive nape of her neck, and feel his other hand tighten around hers. And, just as before, she could feel the intensity of his desire even though it was leashed.

His mouth moved on hers with gentle insistence, inducing a response she had no will or ability to fight. She could feel herself opening to him, her lips parting, and the warmth inside her blossomed into heat when he immediately deepened the kiss. She felt rather than heard a little sound in the back of her throat, a purr of pleasure that would have shocked her if she'd been able to spare a thought for it.

But she didn't think. Her mouth opened wider beneath the increasing pressure of his, and her free hand lifted to his cheek without her conscious volition. It seemed to her that everything else had vanished. There was nothing in the world except them and this heated, fragile moment.

She didn't want it to end. But it did, of course, that moment passing into the next. He lifted his head slowly, his eyes heavy-lidded and darkened with a look so sensual, it made her racing heart skip a beat and caused the heat inside her to flare briefly in response. Her fingers were still touching his cheek, and beneath them she felt the tension of stark control.

His voice revealed the same strain when he spoke. "I want you so much, Dinah. But I promise to take things slowly. You can always stop me with a word. Remember that, please."

She half nodded, still adrift in the heated wash of compelling emotions and sensations. Her hand slowly fell away from him, and she didn't protest when he began leading her toward the door of the storage room—and the world outside.

He held her hand all the way to her office.

Several days passed, busy ones for Dinah—and for everyone else at the museum. The slow process of converting an outdated security system continued. Wolfe was in and out, sometimes clearly harassed but usually his rather laconic self, and Morgan dealt briskly with the myriad details of her job.

Dinah continued with her own work, spending long hours alone in her office. Her tormentor called twice during those days. He didn't ask her to do anything, but simply repeated variations of the threats he'd been making since the beginning.

She didn't tell Max, partly because she knew it would upset him, and partly because she was able to remain relatively calm herself. That whispery voice still made her feel cold and dredged up painful memories, but she found she could handle the emotions because she felt more in control. Less alone. Being with Max made it surprisingly easy to face the threat of her faceless tormentor, and despite the calls her sense of safety increased daily.

Besides that, Max had begun what she could only define to herself as a courtship, and thoughts of any other men were seldom on her mind.

As promised, Max was taking things slowly. He didn't hesitate to touch her now, casual touches that sometimes led to gentle kisses, which often became heated ones. He never went farther than that, and was always the one to stop. Dinah was conscious of his control, and as time passed she developed a solid trust in that. There was absolutely nothing in him to remind her of violence or force, and nothing to trigger fear or panic in her.

As her trust in him deepened, her fear of the physical side of a relationship with him faded until it was a ghostly thing, not quite conquered but not the wound it had been. He made her feel desired without feeling pressured. Her body forgot pain with a new and exciting knowledge of pleasure.

It occurred to her only gradually that in a few short days he had become a vitally important—even necessary—part of her life. The realization sparked a number of emotions in her, most of them based on uncertainty. He hadn't mentioned the future, nor any kind of long-term commitment beyond the fact of his desire for her. Though he had used endearments more than once, she had no idea if that was unusual for him, or if it meant anything at all.

Her own instincts as well as observation of him

told her Max wasn't a man to take any kind of relationship lightly, but that didn't guarantee he had thoughts of permanence. The question was, could she allow herself to go forward without a clear understanding of where it would lead? And what was it that *she* wanted—a relationship with him, or only the peace and safety of the haven he had provided for her?

Dinah didn't have the answers, and there was only a week left of the time she had promised Max. What would happen when that time was up? She couldn't stay with him indefinitely, not if her reason for living in his penthouse was to have sanctuary. She couldn't hide with him, it would be cheating both of them, and quite likely cripple whatever chance she had of rebuilding her self-confidence and independence. Sooner or later, she would have to take charge of her own life again, even if that meant running—or finding the courage to face the threat against her without Max's protection.

In the meantime, all she could do was grapple with her own thoughts and emotions.

On Thursday, Max asked her if she would attend a party with him the following evening. It was being hosted by a friend of his whom he wanted Dinah to meet, a man who was a very influential patron and collector in the art world. The party was a benefit to raise money for a struggling art school in the city, and according to the society pages the elite of San Francisco was expected to attend.

Dinah was a little nervous about it. She didn't come from a poor background, but her average upbringing in Boston hadn't prepared her to enter the kind of circles in which Max moved—in more ways than one. She had a brief discussion with Morgan the next morning, and at lunchtime the two women left the museum together to do a little shopping.

Max, who had unobtrusively made certain Dinah was never alone outside the museum, didn't object to the trip when she told him about it. He did, however, provide a car and driver for them. The reminder that there was still the possibility of a threat against Dinah didn't unsettle her, partly because her mind was occupied with more immediate concerns and partly because she found it difficult to be worried about anything in Morgan's vibrant, cheerful presence.

"I think," Morgan said decisively in the second shop they'd entered, "this has your name written all over it." She had waved the salesclerk away, and she and Dinah were standing alone together beside a display of colorful evening dresses.

Dinah eyed the dress her new friend was holding up, and said doubtfully, "Silver? It's awfully . . . noticeable."

There was a good deal of understanding in Morgan's amber eyes, but she said in a brisk tone, "I went to this bash last year, and I can tell you all the women dress to the teeth. Believe me, you'll see at least a dozen women with sequins *and* feathers." She smiled suddenly. "I can also tell you that Max gets attention wherever he goes—and looking your best is a very effective kind of armor."

Dinah understood the subtle warning, and wondered for the first time if jealous eyes would watch her tonight because she was on Max's arm. Taking the glittery silver dress from Morgan and examining it more closely, she said, "Did you know Max before you began working for him?"

"We met for the first time months ago when he hired me as the director of Mysteries Past," Morgan replied. "But I'd seen him and, of course, knew who he was. I've done administrative work for another art museum as well as a foundation based here in San

Francisco, so I tend to be on the guest list for the benefits and parties connected to the art world."

"Will you be there tonight?"

"Yes, although I hadn't planned to be. Two hours after I told Max I wasn't going, Wolfe asked if I'd go with him."

Dinah looked up quickly. "Wolfe? I hadn't realized— that is—"

Morgan gave her rich chuckle. "No, there's nothing between Wolfe and me—or likely to be. He'd drive me crazy with those brooding silences of his, and I'd no doubt madden *him* talking all the time. I'm sure you've noticed I talk a lot."

Dinah couldn't help but smile. Since Morgan usually carried on about six different subjects at once, it was probably true that a man given to taciturnity would be driven to murder her within a week.

Taking the smile as assent, Morgan nodded. "Yeah. Well, anyway, I consider Wolfe an escort tonight, and nothing more. As for his reasons, I have a feeling Max wanted him to go and suggested he escort me."

"Why? I mean, why does Max want Wolfe at the party?"

"Art collectors," Morgan replied succinctly. "The place will be crawling with them. Since Wolfe is ultimately responsible for the security of the exhibit, and since it's fairly certain only collectors would be interested in so many pieces that would be impossible to fence, the more Wolfe learns about San Francisco's art crowd, the better."

"Reasonable," Dinah agreed.

Morgan nodded again. "And, since Wolfe will be more or less working tonight, I gather that's why I'm to be his date. I'll be understanding if he decides to leave with somebody else. Unlike, I imagine, one of his usual blondes would be."

"Does he have many?" Dinah asked, a little amused by the phrasing.

"Well, he's been in and out of town for the past few months, and I've yet to see him with the same blonde twice. At first, I thought they *were* the same—Barbie dolls, all legs and hair—but then I realized they were different. Slightly different, anyway. The last one drove a Porsche, and the current one—unless he's changed already—drives a little blue Mustang."

"You tell them apart by their cars?"

"It's the best way. Wolfe has a rental since he's based in New York, and he must be saving a bundle on his expense account since all his women seem to drive him places. If you catch him coming or going at the museum, you'll see what I mean." Morgan shook her head. "Talk about brothers being total opposites. But they're half brothers, so maybe that explains it."

"You mean Wolfe and Max are—?"

"Yeah. The same mother. I haven't met her yet, although I hear she's pretty amazing. Max once told me he was absolutely terrified of her—but he was smiling."

Dinah was more than a little surprised by information she hadn't even guessed, and Morgan seemed to sense that.

"Since Wolfe wasn't raised here, I doubt many people know. I found out more or less by accident. Anybody can see he and Max are close, so it doesn't seem to have affected them much to have been raised apart by their fathers. Or if it did affect their childhoods, as adults they don't seem to carry scars—or grudges. With different last names, maybe it's easier not to have to explain the situation. Or maybe they have a reason. They may be keeping quiet about it now just because Wolfe is heading security for the exhibit. I know Max asked specifically for Wolfe when Lloyd's said they'd have to send a man to oversee security. Maybe it's—oh, I don't know—personal preference not to mention they happen to be half brothers."

Dinah made a mental note to bring it up with Max, mostly because she wanted to know if it *was* something generally kept quiet.

"Anyway, they're quite different when it comes to ladies," Morgan added, "which is why I think you should go try on this dress."

"Is there a connection I'm missing?" Dinah wondered.

Morgan chuckled. "Let me put it this way. I doubt any of Wolfe's blondes would be surprised if he showed up with a new one on his arm, because he changes them as regular as clockwork. Max, on the other hand, is rather famous for not giving the society gossip columns anything interesting to dissect. He tends to arrive at parties solo—and leaves the same way. To the absolute fury, I might add, of a number of ladies who've been after him for years."

Slowly, Dinah said, "Which is why I should try on this dress?"

"Forewarned is forearmed. You won't be walking into a cage full of tigers, but I'd advise you to brace yourself for a few . . . gently extended claws. If you know what I mean."

"Wonderful," Dinah murmured.

"You'll handle them," Morgan said confidently. "When you walk into Leo Cassady's house tomorrow night, I'm going to enjoy watching a number of faces turn pea-green."

Max had to take a phone call shortly after he and Dinah arrived back at his apartment from the museum a little after five o'clock on Friday night, which gave her time to get ready before he did. The party began at seven, and since there would be food they weren't planning to have dinner beforehand.

The den was deserted when Dinah finished dressing. Max wasn't in his office, and since his bedroom door had been closed she assumed he was changing.

Mrs. Perry had already left to have dinner and see a musical with friends and wasn't expected back at the apartment until late.

Dinah placed her wrap and purse on one of the chairs and went over to stare out the window, fighting her nervousness. She knew she looked her best—Morgan had definitely been right about the silver dress—but Dinah's self-confidence and self-esteem had never quite recovered from what had happened in Boston.

The last days with Max had made her feel better about herself in many subtle ways, but deep wounds healed very slowly, and hers had been reopened too recently to be completely healed so soon even by his touch.

His touch . . .

That worried her most of all. She had run before, a response she had always seen as an act of cowardice no matter how she'd tried to defend it to herself. Was she staying with Max now because of a different kind of cowardice? How could she really know how she felt about him when her motivations for staying were so tangled? Was she using him for sanctuary and for the healing wizardry of his touch?

"Lord, you're beautiful."

She half turned from the window, watching as Max came toward her slowly. The husky words made her heart beat faster, and seeing how ruggedly handsome he looked in the elegant tux had a profound effect on her ability to breathe normally. A little desperately, she told herself she could hardly feel like this if all her motives were selfish ones. Could she?

"Thank you," she murmured when he reached her.

He smiled slightly as he took one of her hands in his, looking at her very intently. "Beautiful—and worried. You've been fighting demons, haven't you, Dinah?"

"A few," she admitted.

"I wish I could fight them for you."

Dinah hesitated, then said, "That's part of the problem. I *am* letting you fight some of them."

Max lifted his free hand and cupped her cheek, his smile fading a little. "Are you sure about that?"

"You said I'd be a coward if I ran. Maybe I'm being more of a coward by staying with you—and letting you fight the demons for me. I'm not *doing* anything, Max, I'm just pretending nothing happened. I'm not trying to fight that man, not trying to make him pay for what he did to me. I haven't even let myself get angry at him. All I'm doing is staying in this safe place you've given me—and I haven't even asked if you're any closer to finding him."

As always, Max intuitively went straight to the heart of her uncertainty. And he asked the question as if he wanted *her* answer, not as if he was uncertain himself. "Is that why you're staying with me? So I'll fight your battles?"

"I don't know," she whispered. "But if it's true, I shouldn't be here. A relationship shouldn't be a haven, a place to hide. You've made it so easy for me to be with you, I'm seeing that only now, questioning it only now. How will I ever be whole again if I don't learn to fight for myself?"

Max looked at her upturned face for several moments, his thumb lightly brushing her cheekbone, his expression grave. "Sweetheart, you aren't hiding—you're healing. There's a big difference. None of us can fight an outside force *until* we're whole."

Dinah frowned a little, trying to understand what he meant, and he nodded slightly.

"Think about it. What happened to you in Boston was worsened by the fact there was no safe place for you to heal. That animal got in with a police car parked at the curb and locks on your doors. He shattered your faith in safety. Because you never felt safe after that, you never healed. Running didn't help, because when you ran here, another animal got in."

"But I feel safe with you," she said slowly.

"And you're healing. Dinah, we all need a haven, a safe place where we can recover from blows and gather our strength. Your haven is this apartment, the museum, the safeguards to protect you. It isn't me, or our relationship. Don't confuse two very different things. I'd fight all your battles if I could, but I can't. You wouldn't let me, you're too strong for that. The fact that you're worried about it now only proves what I'm saying. You want to fight for yourself, and you will. When you're healed. When you're ready."

It made sense to Dinah—and made her feel better. But there was still a worry, and she had to voice it aloud. "You're helping me to heal. Apart from giving me a safe place, and time, you're helping just by . . . being you."

He smiled. "Is that bad?"

"It's confusing." She met his gaze as directly as she could. "How do I know that what I—I feel for you isn't based on gratitude?"

It was the first time she had admitted feeling anything for him, and Max went very still as he gazed down at her. She was so beautiful, the sexy dress clinging to her slender body, her fiery hair framing the delicate features of her lovely face. He had wanted her for so long, and so intensely, it felt as if he had waited for her forever. But her haunting sapphire eyes were shadowed, and her lips trembled. She looked so vulnerable, he knew he could lose everything if his own response was wrong—or less than honest.

After a moment, he said huskily, "I feel gratitude. Gratitude that you trusted me enough to stay with me. Gratitude that you came into my life, when I'd given up hope of finding you. I can't see anything wrong in that, Dinah. Haven't you realized yet? I love you."

It was the last thing she had expected to hear, and for an instant Dinah was so stunned, she could only stare up at him. Love? He loved her? Almost whispering, she said, "You've known me barely a week, how can you—?"

"I asked you once if you believed in love at first sight; you said no. I believe in it because I know it's possible." He pulled her into his arms, holding her close. "I love you, Dinah. I've loved you since the first time I saw you."

"It isn't possible." In the dark subconscious of her mind, where the most primitive emotions lurked, were Dinah's deepest scars. That was where a rapist had done the most damage to her. The irrational shame, the conviction that she would never be clean again, the belief she was damaged, unworthy somehow. The soul-deep trauma of having been a victim of violence, and the terrible anguish of a woman made utterly helpless by the brutality of a man.

All of those bleak emotions crowded into her awareness as if a dam had shattered with his words. She wanted to twist away from him, to run and hide herself from him. It wasn't rational or logical; it wasn't a thinking response. All she knew in that moment was that she didn't deserve to be loved.

"Dinah."

She blinked up at him, realizing only then how stiff her body was. She wondered what was in her face to make his go so pale, to make his eyes darken almost to black. Her hands were on his broad chest. She had pushed herself back, and was holding him away from her. "It isn't possible," she repeated in a thin voice. "I don't deserve—"

"Stop it." He bit out the command, his voice very soft yet fierce. "Don't you ever say that. Don't even think it. *It wasn't your fault.* What happened to you was a horrible thing, Dinah, but it didn't make you dirty. It didn't make you less than you were before. You deserve everything good life has to offer, *especially* love."

Six

Confusion swept in on the heels of her ragged, painful emotions, and Dinah stopped resisting him. He pulled her close once more, holding her against him. She hadn't realized those feelings had lurked inside her, and confronting them now was one of the hardest things she'd ever had to do.

"I love you, Dinah," Max said.

Memories crashed into her mind, making her shudder in his arms. Memories of what had occurred in her supposedly safe bedroom in Boston. Darkness all around, the very absence of light triggering primal horror that had made what happened even worse. The fear and pain, the awful degradation and smothering knowledge of total helplessness. And, worst of all, the terror of knowing that the violent man using her could snuff out her life as easily as he'd swat a fly, and that there was *nothing* she could do to stop him.

Then, later, the shame—and the guilt. The way people had looked at her. The whispering. Even her brother . . . Even Glenn had hinted that she must have done something to attract the rapist's attention—or else why had he noticed her in the first place? Later, she had overheard Glenn talking with a friend of his, and he had wondered aloud why she'd had no visible bruises or cuts after the attack, why she apparently hadn't fought the rapist. It just seemed odd, Glenn had said, that the man had gotten into her apartment so easily, bypassing all the alarms and locks—almost as if someone had let him in. . . .

As if someone had let him in.

That was when Dinah had made up her mind to leave Boston, to cut the ties to her past. If even her own brother, the only man she had still trusted, believed that she was somehow at fault for having been raped—and for having survived it—who was on her side? If even Glenn could doubt her word and suspect her of being guilty of lying about what had happened to her, then there was truly nothing left in Boston for her.

It was normal what she was going through, the counselor had told her repeatedly; society made a woman ashamed of being victimized, questioning and doubting her. There was still a tendency to view rape as a sexual attack, provoked by seductive clothing or a provocative attitude, and far too many people still held that a man must have been enticed to commit such a crime—which meant the woman was blamed.

And the guilt Dinah felt, the counselor explained, was a product of having survived such a devastating attack. Another of society's outrageous and outdated burdens imposed on women, the ludicrous belief that there could be a "fate worse than death," and that any woman should sacrifice her life rather than "submit" to rape—and survive it. Not rational or logical, but human emotions seldom were. Like the certainty of not being clean, no matter how often and hard she'd scrubbed herself. Like the conviction that she had been forever marked, terribly diminished by what had been taken from her.

Not just virginity. But innocence. Trust.

"I love you, Dinah."

No matter how well she healed, the counselor had told her gently, her perception of life had been forever altered. She would always be more aware of dark corners and deserted areas. Turning out a light would never become the unthinking act it had once been. Nightmares would hold more violence, because she knew what violence was now. Strangers would be measured warily, and trust given with great difficulty. And safety would never, ever, be taken for granted again.

That was the stain violence left on the soul.

Dinah was fighting it now, struggling to force intellect to overcome emotion. Trying to convince herself that she wasn't dirty, or unworthy, or undeserving only because she'd had the tragic misfortune to be attacked by a brutal man. It hadn't been her fault. . . . It *hadn't*. . . .

"I love you."

Finally, the low, intense words sank into her chaotic thoughts like a healing balm. He meant it, she realized, he really meant it. Incredible as she found it, he really loved her. She didn't know, couldn't know, if it would prove to be an enduring love, but he loved her now, and for now it was enough.

Gradually, she stopped shaking. The wounds were still there, but exposed to the light now, and confronted. They didn't hurt so much, didn't tear at her like things with talons and teeth.

She didn't realize she'd been crying for a long time.

When she finally drew away, he wouldn't let her go very far. "I must look like hell," she murmured, brushing away the last of her tears with her fingertips as she looked up at him. Thank heaven for water-and-tear-proof mascara, she thought vaguely. At least she wouldn't look like a panda. "And I've probably ruined your jacket—"

"Never mind my jacket." He was smiling, but still a little pale, as if her silent, fierce struggle had affected him almost as much as it had her. "And you could never be anything but beautiful."

She had to say something. He had told her he loved her, and she had responded with wild disbelief and then a torrent of tears. She couldn't just let his declaration lie there between them as if it didn't matter to her. "Max . . ."

He touched her lips lightly with a finger. "I know you're feeling . . . raw. So am I. Let's give it a little time, all right? Between us, we've kicked your demons out of the dark; that's enough for now."

No longer surprised at his perception, she nodded. But she couldn't leave it at that. "I also feel better," she told him honestly. "Stronger."

"Good. Strong enough to go with me to this party?"

Dinah felt her lips curve into a smile as she realized that kicking demons out of the dark had one immediate benefit: Elegant felines in sequins and feathers no longer had the power to make her nervous. "I think I can handle it," she said. "Give me ten minutes to fix my face, and I'll be ready."

"There's absolutely nothing wrong with your face," Max said seriously. "The pink lids make your eyes look even more like sapphires."

Dinah had to laugh, but she lost no time in retreating to her bedroom to make repairs.

If there were any catty comments directed at Dinah that evening, she didn't notice them. Thinking back later, she decided that there hadn't been any, partly because Max hardly left her side and gave no one an opportunity to extend feline claws. He didn't stick close as if he felt she needed his protection, but made it obvious to anyone who cared to look that he simply didn't want to be anywhere else.

As for Dinah, she felt only a mild, detached interest in the glittering crowd filling Leo Cassady's beautiful Sea Cliff mansion; most of her attention was focused on Max. He was making no attempt whatsoever to hide or disguise his feelings, and Dinah was coping with the shock and wonder of being cherished.

It was . . . strange. Part of her simply couldn't believe it, yet she had to. Max loved her. She knew him well enough by now to feel sure he wasn't lying, or trying to deceive her in any way. If she knew anything at all about him, it was that the core of his personality was a deep and unique honesty. He would never lie about what he felt. And, as the evening wore on, her certainty in that grew ever stronger.

They had eaten and danced, and Max had shown her many of the exquisite paintings and other pieces in Leo's impressive collection. She had noted without comment the presence of several unobtrusive plainclothes guards dressed as formally as the guests as they kept an eye on the valuables, and she took it for granted that the display cases and paintings were protected by an invisible, but no doubt extensive, security system. Even the reminder of possible thieves, or the beauty of art, however, couldn't distract her attention very long.

Max held her hand or placed one of his at the small of her back constantly, as if the physical contact was necessary to him. His gray eyes were warm and unshadowed when they rested on her, and his voice, his incredible voice, tugged at her heart and senses each time he spoke, even if the words were casual.

Time passed, for Dinah, in a haze of tentative, but growing, happiness.

She had been introduced to a number of people and had, she trusted, replied suitably, but she didn't really talk to anyone but Max until Morgan appeared at her side a couple of hours after they'd arrived. Max was standing on Dinah's left, talking to Leo Cassady—who had turned out to be a very handsome and charming man about ten years Max's senior and was obviously popular with both men and women alike. They were in a lovely foyer graced by exquisite paintings, with the bulk of the guests dancing in the ballroom just a few feet away.

"I don't know why I bothered to warn you," Morgan said somewhat wryly as she appeared beside Dinah. "Every woman in this house knew Max was out of circulation the moment you two walked in. It's obvious they've decided to admit defeat without even a token struggle."

With her left hand held securely in Max's, Dinah felt too content to argue the point—even if she'd wanted to. Instead, with a smile at the other woman, who was absolutely radiant in a gown of pure gold, Dinah said, "Where's Wolfe?"

"He abandoned me for a blonde," Morgan replied without rancor, and then giggled. "I suppose I should have warned him that the one he's dancing with now is a shark with a full set of teeth, but he's a big boy. I decided to let him fend for himself."

Leo took a step sideways to better see Morgan, and it was obvious he had overheard her remark. "Are you talking about our Nyssa, Morgan?" he asked with a gleam of laughter in his eyes.

"The very same," she replied promptly. "Not only does she have a habit of snaring my dates without mercy, but she's tried twice tonight to get my promise that she'll be allowed to see Mysteries Past even before the private showing."

Leo lifted a brow. "I should have thought she would have asked Max," he commented.

Morgan grinned. "She's tried everything but blackmail on Max for months, and finally admitted defeat. She told me so. So now it's my turn. If she tries to bribe me, Max, and offers big bucks, I'm going to be real tempted."

Amused, Max said, "Give me a chance to better any offer she makes."

"You're on." Then, sobering, Morgan said, "She

also asked me if you'd consider selling any piece of the collection. I thought everyone knew that answer."

"She knows," Max responded. "She just doesn't give up easily."

"She's a collector?" Dinah asked, looking through the open doors into the ballroom to watch Wolfe dancing with a tall and stunning blonde of about thirty-five.

"Rabid," Leo confirmed. "When she buried Lewis Armstrong ten years ago, shortly after their honeymoon, he left her a respectable collection of paintings and a nice little nest egg. She's been very smart with the money—and very ambitious in doing all she can to build on the collection." His eyes gleamed suddenly. "She's also extremely talented in the various arts of . . . persuasion."

"Do you know that firsthand?" Morgan asked with a lurking smile.

In a meditative tone, Leo said, "I turned down an offer of thirty thousand for my Greek chalice." He smiled, said, "Excuse me," and strolled away.

Dinah looked up at Max, who seemed amused, and then at Morgan, who was chuckling. "The Greek chalice?" she inquired.

"Nyssa has it," Morgan said. "You see, Max, I *told* you when Nyssa started bragging about her Greek chalice a couple of months ago that it was Leo's. She says she got it for ten thousand—and you can bet she bartered the rest."

"Morgan," Max said in mild protest.

"Oh, Max, she doesn't care what people say about her. And, to give her credit, she's honest about it. Brutally honest. She told me herself that the brief affair with Jack Stuart everybody made such a fuss about last winter was only because she wanted to get her hands on his Renoir—and she got it at a bargain-basement price. Tell her she earned something on her back, and she considers it a compliment."

Dinah couldn't help but wonder if the "everything but blackmail" Nyssa had tried on Max had included her reputed talents in the bedroom, and tried to shake off the thought. She had no right to feel jealous over something that may or may not have happened before she'd even met Max—and was more than a little shocked to realize she felt jealousy at all.

"Be that as it may," Max was saying calmly to Morgan, "you know very well how exaggerated stories get when collectors start comparing value and price."

"It's a vicious cycle," Morgan agreed solemnly, then set her champagne glass aside and added, "Excuse me, I think I'll go and rescue Wolfe—whether he needs it or not. See you."

"Has she mentioned Quinn to you?" Dinah asked, watching the other woman disappear into the ballroom.

"Not since our meeting the other day," Max replied, looking down at her. "Why?"

Dinah hesitated, then shook her head. "No reason."

"Dance, Dinah?"

"I've love to." She was a little surprised, though, when Max led her through the ballroom and then out onto the wide terrace. There were lanterns and a number of comfortable seats, obviously for any guests who chose to escape the crowded ballroom. It was a cool night, but not uncomfortably so, and there was no wind or fog to discourage anyone. There were already a number of people on the terrace, but it was such a large area there was still a feeling of intimacy when Max drew Dinah into his arms.

The music from the ballroom had slowed to a lazy, almost throbbing beat, and she was highly conscious of it as they moved slowly together in perfect step.

"Why did you ask if Morgan had mentioned Quinn?" Max asked quietly.

Gazing up at his deceptively hard face in the golden glow of the lamps, Dinah had to force herself to concentrate on words. "Well . . . she encountered an internationally infamous cat burglar while a museum was being robbed, and that's quite a situation. Something to talk about, I'd think. Morgan talks about practically everything under the sun, but she hasn't talked about that. It just struck me as odd, that's all." Dinah hesitated, then added, "Maybe Quinn made more of an impression on Morgan than she wants to admit to us. There's an aura of romance clinging to that kind of larger-than-life character, even if you consider him a criminal."

After a moment, Max said, "I hope not. It's doubtful she'll ever see him again."

"I don't know," Dinah said wryly. "We seem to have thieves all over the place. In a city stuffed with art and valuables. Max, are you sure it's the right time to open your exhibit?"

He smiled slightly. "I gave my word."

Dinah didn't want to bring up the subject, but she felt an odd compulsion to. "The gang that looted that museum hasn't been caught. Quinn's at large, and they say he's very good at what he does. And what about the thief who was trying to use me? He's still out there somewhere. The lengths he went to . . . he won't give up."

As always, Max seemed to understand what question she was really asking, and that was the one he answered. "I haven't had any luck in finding him. There's almost nothing to go on. The truth is, I may not be able to find him. Will you leave me in a week, Dinah?"

"I don't know," she answered, because that was the truth. "I'm still not sure my reasons for staying are the right ones. I don't want to be dishonest with you, Max."

"There isn't a dishonest bone in your body," he told her.

"I have to be sure. *I* have to," she said with determination. "I have to know I'm not hiding with you."

There was a long silence while they danced slowly, and then Max said, "You haven't given yourself enough time to be certain of anything. We still have a week."

Very conscious of his hand at the small of her back and of how close they were dancing, Dinah whispered, "Maybe it isn't more time that I need. Maybe what I need to know . . . is whether I can heal from what happened two years ago."

Max stopped dancing, but still held her close as he gazed down at her upturned face. He knew what she was saying, and the response of his body was so immediate and intense, it was almost impossible for him to think of anything else. But he had to think, because he was still convinced that if he allowed his hunger for her to drive him into a too hasty step, he would lose her forever.

With an effort that made his throat hurt, he managed to keep his voice steady. "Dinah, love, I hope you know how much I want you. But even more than that, I don't want either of us to make a mistake. I love you, and I'll wait as long as it takes for you to be sure you want me. I don't want you to feel you have to do anything you aren't ready for, just because some imagined deadline is looming."

"You said it," she reminded him. "We have a week."

Max shook his head. "A week you promised me, because you couldn't say you'd stay with me indefinitely. Not a deadline, sweetheart. I hope you'll be with me for the next forty or fifty years."

Dinah felt the strangest sensation then. It was hot and cold, excited and panicked, desperate and fearful. And there was a feeling of unreality, of being poised on the brink of something so important she was almost afraid to move for fear of shattering the moment. Then she heard herself speak, and realized that her instincts were certain of what her confused mind and tangled emotions still doubted.

"I don't know what lovemaking feels like," she said a bit unsteadily. "But I do know I'll never be able to love until I find out. I'll never be able to let myself love until I can trust even when I'm . . . that vulnerable. I want to love you, Max. I've never wanted anything more in my life. I don't need a week to be sure of that, or even an hour. All I need . . . is you."

Max was torn. He wanted her so badly, and because he loved her he honestly believed he could, with that love, heal the wounds another man had inflicted on her. What he was unsure of was whether Dinah was truly ready to put that to the test. If they began making love and either fear or panic made her pull away from him, the fragile bond of her trust would be broken forever. To Dinah, it would be a stark failure of her ability to put the past behind her and lead a normal life, a failure from which she might never recover.

But, gazing at her upturned face, what he saw wasn't the resolution of someone determined to take an action whether she was ready or not; what he saw was yearning, a sweet, shy eagerness, and hope.

It almost broke his heart.

He bent his head to kiss her gently, holding the reins of control with all his will. "Let's get out of here," he muttered against her lips.

Dinah didn't notice another soul in the crowded ballroom as he led her back through it and to the front door. All her attention was focused on Max, nobody intruded. Morgan told Dinah, much later, that their determination to be alone together just as fast as they could manage it was about as subtle as neon. But even if Dinah had realized that then, she wouldn't have cared. She was still poised on the brink, all her senses heated and nervous, her emotions silent in waiting, her thoughts fixed totally on the single truth of what she needed.

She realized only later that they barely paused to reclaim their coats, which appeared almost magically, and if Max said their good-byes to their host, she didn't notice it. The house could have gone off like a rocket behind them as they drove away, and she wouldn't have noticed.

Max placed her left hand on his thigh and held it there as he drove, and she couldn't take her eyes off his profile. Like that first day in the park when he had drawn the truth out of her, she felt linked with him, tied in some basic way she couldn't understand but only feel. All evening, they had been in almost constant physical contact, and there had been nothing casual about it. She had the vague awareness that the sustained closeness had enabled her to see what it was she needed to banish the ghosts of the past.

When they reached the apartment building, she walked beside him to the elevator. Curiously enough, she wasn't at all afraid. Nervous, yes, and worried about her own ability to respond when the moment came, but there wasn't even the whisper of fear of Max or of his desire.

He had succeeded in teaching her to trust him despite the odds, and because it was a trust seeded and grown in the rocky ground of doubts and disbelief it was probably the strongest trust of her life. She believed that Max would never intentionally hurt her and, more, that his unusually emphatic nature made even an unintentional hurt virtually impossible. And she believed he loved her.

She was ready to put it to the test, to discover if she could feel desire—and love. Fate, however, in the guise of a stranger, intended she wait at least a little longer.

Max's penthouse occupied the entire top floor of the building, and to gain access to that floor required either a special key or the permission of someone already in the apartment. The same was true of the apartment itself. So, when the elevator doors opened to reveal a tall stranger waiting in the foyer, Dinah's only thought was that Mrs. Perry must have returned and allowed the man to come up. But why had she kept him waiting out here?

Max went still for an instant beside her, and she could have sworn he muttered an oath under his breath, but his voice was as calm as usual when he led her forward and spoke to the man.

"Nice timing."

The man's hazel eyes flicked to Dinah for a moment, and then he looked at Max and said, "We have to talk." His voice was very calm.

Max unlocked the apartment door, and quietly introduced Dinah to Keane Tyler, saying only that he was a friend. Dinah didn't ask for further explanation. She could have, though, since she recognized the quiet man. He had been the driver Max had supplied when she and Morgan had gone shopping. She had believed him no more than a chauffeur then, but now she wondered. Her instincts told her he was no employee, that he and Max were on equal footing.

As soon as they were inside the apartment, she quietly excused herself.

Max's hand immediately tightened around hers. "Dinah, you don't have to—"

"It's all right." Her glance flicked to Keane, then returned to Max. "I have to change anyway." She gently pulled her hand from his, and went down the hall to her bedroom.

Mrs. Perry's bedroom was on the other side of the apartment near the kitchen, and she hadn't appeared when they'd entered the apartment, but there was evidence of her return. As usual, Dinah's bed had been turned down, and the lamp on her nightstand was burning in welcome.

Why had Keane Tyler waited in the foyer?

Dinah thought about that as she undressed and took a shower, choosing to occupy her mind with the puzzle to avoid worrying about the interruption. She wondered suddenly if it had been Keane who'd been at the apartment that first night talking to Max about her. Or it could have been Wolfe.

Then she had the peculiar idea that mentioning it to whichever one *hadn't* been there would be a mistake.

Out in the living room, Max had discarded his coat, jacket, and tie, and absently set his gold cuff links on the bar as he rolled his sleeves up.

"I really am sorry, Max."

He glanced over at Keane. "Drink?"

"No, thanks. I won't be staying long."

Max fixed a brandy for himself and finished it in one swallow, the only outward sign of inner disturbance. He pushed the empty snifter aside, then leaned on the bar and studied his visitor. "What's up?"

Keane slowly approached the bar, not speaking until he reached it. "You wanted me to check with NCIC. The Crime Information Center spit out a pretty long list of thieves whose M.O. is to pressure or blackmail insiders into helping them."

"You no longer consider Dinah a threat?" Max asked, rather mildly.

Keane winced, but met the steady gaze squarely. "Okay, I was wrong about her. I'm sorry I jumped to conclusions." He hesitated, then added, "After what she went through, it's no wonder she couldn't fight this bastard."

Max half nodded. "I'm glad you realize that."

"I may be cynical," Keane said, "but I'm not stupid—or unfeeling. I'm also one of San Francisco's finest, which means I want to get the son of a bitch almost as bad as you do."

After a moment, Max said, "How many names on that list?"

"When I started out, over two dozen. It took me time, but I was gradually able to eliminate all but a dozen, because the others are either confirmed as being a long way from San Francisco, or else their targets never include jewelry or artworks. Of the remaining dozen, I eliminated another eight because they're small-timers without the brains or the guts to attempt any score as large as your collection."

"And the remaining four?"

"One was released from prison a few months ago, and is reported to be towing the line. I checked him out personally, and I doubt he's our man. He has a new wife and a steady job, and his parole officer thinks he's gone straight. I crossed him off the list. That leaves three. Of those, two specialize in jewelry stores and habitually focus on easily fenced merchandise. Neither has been tied in with a single museum robbery, and neither has any experience with art."

"Who is he?"

Keane shoved his hands into the pockets of his coat and sighed. "It's not as easy as that, Max. Narrowing the list to one name doesn't necessarily mean he's guilty. From what you told me, Dinah won't be able to identify him since she never saw his face. And he hasn't gotten into the museum, so we can't pin robbery or attempted robbery on him. There are no outstanding warrants with his name on them. I can't find any evidence against him for any crime—and I've looked, believe me."

Conversationally, Max said, "Why won't you tell me who he is?"

"Because you might recognize his name." Keane paused, then added softly, "I never point a loaded gun unless it's under my control." He watched Max smile, and thought, not for the first time, that the last man on earth he would choose for an enemy would be this one. Thank God they were friends.

"Are you so sure I'd go after him?"

"Positive. You aren't entirely rational where Dinah's concerned, are you?"

Instead of answering, Max said, "If you don't plan to tell me, then what do you intend to do about him?"

Keane mentally braced himself. "Unless he makes another attempt at the museum, there's nothing I can do. Max, he's never even been convicted of a felony. Suspected—yes, of a list as long as your arm. But never convicted. Unless he tries again, or unless Dinah can positively identify him as the man who terrorized her, I can't touch him."

Max gazed across the room toward the windows, his face expressionless. He knew Keane well enough to realize that it was useless to argue with him, but he was also very conscious of his own implacable determination to see to it that at least one of the brutal men who had hurt Dinah paid for his crimes.

Slowly, he said, "Do you think he will try to get at the collection again?"

Keane had obviously given the matter considerable thought, because his answer was immediate. "According to his files, he always stuck his neck out for a big score—and they don't come any bigger than the Bannister collection. He'll try again." Keane hesitated, then said, "He may even try to use Dinah."

Max's face hardened. "I know. I've known it all along. As long as she's connected to the museum, she's at risk. But I can't ask her to give up the job. She's already worried that by staying with me, she's hiding from reality. In fact . . ."

"In fact?"

"He may have called her at the museum since I brought her here, but, if he has, Dinah hasn't mentioned it. I think she'd tell me if he wanted her to do something else, but she might not tell me if he's still calling just to terrorize her."

Keane sighed. "He probably is. I wish I could say it's unlikely, but I can't see this guy not trying to use Dinah. The closest he ever came to being caught was because he was unbelievably arrogant. He was absolutely positive he could control his tool—and it was a woman that time too. If he believes that Dinah being here is your idea rather than hers, and that it's personal and has nothing to do with the exhibit, he may well feel confident, even now, that he can control her through fear."

"I won't use Dinah to bait a trap," Max said flatly. "The police used her once before, in Boston, and then they let that animal get to her. I'd give up every piece of the collection before I'd ask her to take that risk once more."

"I know. I just wanted you to be prepared in case he pressures Dinah again. Because it is likely, Max." Keane shook his head slightly. "I hope I'm wrong, but I don't think I am. Your collection is worth just about any risk—and his only chance is Dinah. He hasn't forgotten that."

Seven

It was nearly an hour after she'd gone to her room that Dinah ventured out again. She had listened at her door for a moment and, hearing no voices from the living room, hoped that Keane Tyler had gone. She wasn't much interested in whatever the meeting had been about. Right now, all that was on her mind was Max . . . and possibilities.

She had put on her prettiest nightgown. It was made of sheer royal blue silk, and it whispered as she moved slowly down the hallway to the living room. She couldn't believe she was doing this. A week ago, she would have said it would be impossible. It had, in fact, required a considerable amount of courage for her to leave her bedroom and go to Max. She had been able to do it because it was what she wanted, and because she wanted him to be certain this was her choice.

In the soft light and silence of the living room, he was standing by the window, gazing over the lights of the city spread out below. He was informal now, his shirtsleeves rolled up and collar open. The stark whiteness of his shirt against the darkness outside the window made him appear even more ruggedly powerful than usual, and her pulse quickened in response.

She moved toward him silently until she was a few feet away, then stopped. "Max?"

He turned to face her, a glitter of heat instantly igniting in the gray eyes that traveled slowly from her shining hair to her bare feet and then back to her face. His low voice was even deeper than usual, almost a soft growl when he said, "Interruptions sometimes bring second thoughts."

Dinah understood what he was saying. It was why he hadn't gone to her. "I don't have second thoughts," she murmured, taking another step toward him. "Do you?"

Max closed the distance between them in two strides, his hands lifting to hold her bare shoulders. It was an almost electric touch. She could feel the heat of his body, so close now, and was incredibly conscious of his enormous strength despite the gentleness of his hands. But it didn't frighten her, because she had developed an absolute trust in his ability to leash that strength.

If he was still not quite sure she was ready for this, it seemed he could no longer question her determination. He murmured her name, a rough, aching sound, and bent his head to capture her lips.

For the first time, Dinah's response wasn't veiled by the guarded, nervous part of her. Her arms slid up around his neck, her mouth opened beneath the hungry pressure of his, and her body melted against his in a longing so intense, there was no room in her for anything else. The warmth his kisses always evoked in her was nothing compared to the explosion of heat that detonated inside her then, sending hot pleasure throbbing along her nerve endings in sensations she had never even imagined herself capable of feeling.

This was right. It *felt* right.

Max seemed totally absorbed in kissing her, his

hard mouth slanting over hers to deepen the contact, the small possession of his tongue slow and incredibly sensuous. His arms were wrapped around her, holding her tightly against him, and she could feel the heat and power of his body triggering a strange new hunger inside her. She had felt the beginnings of desire in his arms before, but this . . . this was need, the recognition of an imperative too strong to resist.

Dinah didn't even try. She rose on her tiptoes, fitting herself more intimately to his body, and a groan rumbled in his chest as her yielding loins nestled against his throbbing flesh. For an instant he held her even tighter, one hand sliding down her back to press her hips harder against him. The desire in his kiss intensified, becoming so hot she felt branded by it, and she kissed him almost wildly in return. Then he drew back to give her a fierce look, a look she was dimly aware of answering with the silent yearning she was helpless to hide.

With a low, rough sound, Max bent and lifted her into his arms, handling her slight weight with no strain at all as he carried her through the apartment to his bedroom. As in her room, the covers had been turned back on his wide bed and a lamp burned on the nightstand; she didn't notice more than that. Being carried by him with such ease was an unsettling experience, both exciting and a little alarming; she didn't feel so much helpless as peculiarly fragile. She couldn't take her eyes off his face, as if she needed to memorize him feature by feature.

He kicked the door shut when he carried her in, then stopped beside the bed and set her gently on her feet. His eyes were darkened, burning, the lids heavy—a sensual look that made her racing heart skip a beat. There was something primitive in the tautness of his face, something so inherently male that everything in her that was female responded instantly. If his kiss had branded her, that intent, overwhelming need in his eyes and expression marked her in another way, in an even deeper place in her soul.

"Dinah . . ." he whispered roughly, framing her face with unsteady hands. He kissed her again and again, deep, drugging kisses that made waves of pleasure spread throughout her body.

She touched his chest, her thumb finding the opening of his shirt and the thick, soft black hair growing there. Without thought, she fumbled with several buttons until both her hands could push aside the material and touch him, and a little purr of triumph escaped her as her fingers slid into the curling dark hair. She hadn't known she was a tactile creature, but touching him like this brought her a dizzying excitement and pleasure. He felt wonderful. Her fingers probed compulsively, delighting in what she found. There was little give to him. Under his skin was strong muscle and solid bone, the very hardness of him quintessentially masculine.

It made her aware of her lesser size and strength, but not in a negative way. Instead, she felt primitive emotions of her own surge inside her, a woman's instinctive recognition of her power over a more powerful being. Feeling his heart pounding beneath her touch, his body tremble, she realized for the first time that, although a man could hold a woman powerless with the sheer force of his physical strength, she could hold him in an even more vulnerable condition if he desired her.

All those thoughts filtered into her mind, but she didn't bother to examine them, being too caught up in what was happening between them. She was barely aware that Max had shrugged out of his shirt and tossed it aside, because his lips were on her throat and the sensations were extraordinary. She felt him move, and realized dimly that he had sat down on the side of the bed and drawn her between his knees. His lips trailed down her throat and paused at her collarbone, his tongue darting into the sensitive hollow there, and a little gasp left her parted lips as her head fell back to allow him more room to explore.

His broad shoulders were under her hands, and he was hard there as well, muscles and tendons unyielding to her probing touch. She slid her fingers up the strong column of his neck and into his thick hair, her eyes closed as all her other senses focused on what he was doing. His hands were on her hips, slowly drawing the long skirt of the nightgown up, and his mouth trailed fire downward to the deep V neckline.

His mouth settled between her breasts just as his hands slipped beneath the silk of her nightgown to touch her naked flesh, and a muted sound of surprise and pleasure escaped Dinah. His hands were slightly rough and warm, touching her hips and then moving gently over her bottom in a starkly intimate caress, and his mouth was exploring the inner curves of her breasts in a slow, heated way that was maddening.

She could feel her breasts swelling, feel the nipples prickle in a sudden, sharp hunger that was painful. She couldn't catch her breath, and her heart was racing so wildly, she knew he could feel it, perhaps even hear it. Unconsciously, she removed her hands from him long enough to push the straps of her nightgown off her shoulders. She couldn't breathe at all when his mouth moved slowly toward a still-covered nipple. And her body arched in a helpless response when he brushed the silk aside and drew the hard bud into his mouth.

All the strength drained from her legs in a rush as burning pleasure spread outward through her body like ripples in a pool, and she half collapsed against him. The hot, wet caress satisfied her hunger and yet drove it ever higher, tormenting her body even as it pleasured. She didn't think she could bear it.

"Max . . . please . . ." She pleaded, not even sure

what she was asking for. All she knew was that the fire he had ignited inside her was burning out of control, and she was afraid it would consume her.

He continued the torture a few moments longer, concentrating his attentions on her other breast while his hands continued to stroke beneath the skirt of her nightgown. Then he eased her back just enough so that he could rise to his feet again. His lips trailed back up over her breastbone, her throat, then covered her mouth in a fierce kiss of pure need. Dinah responded with the same fiery craving, her mouth wild under his.

She moaned a protest when he broke off the kiss, her eyes opening finally to stare up into his burning ones. Even more than usual, she was trapped, and the pull of his gaze was so intense she actually cried out a little—not in protest but in wonder. Then he was drawing the nightgown up over her head, and she lifted her arms instinctively to be free of it. He dropped the garment carelessly to the floor, raking her naked body with eyes so fierce she could feel the touch of them.

"Dinah . . . my God, you're beautiful . . ." he growled, a deep, rumbling sound that seemed to come from the very core of him, and something in it was so primitive, it touched all her instincts as if it were an ancient mating call her very cells recognized.

Before Dinah could say anything, or become fully aware of her nakedness, he lifted her and placed her in the middle of the wide bed. He came down beside her immediately, his mouth on hers and his hand surrounding a swollen breast. The hot, sweet tension inside Dinah wound tighter and tighter, gripping her body in a merciless coil of building need until she couldn't be still, couldn't breathe, couldn't even ask him why he was tormenting her this way.

His hand on her aching breast, the rough pad of his thumb brushing her tight nipple rhythmically, sent bursts of heat through her and yanked a moan from her throat. It was incredible, what he was making her feel. She couldn't control her body anymore. When his mouth closed over her throbbing nipple and his hand slid slowly down over her quivering belly, her legs parted for him without hesitation.

What little breath remained in her caught in her throat, tangling with a wild cry she couldn't hold back. All her senses seemed to overload, strained beyond bearing, at the raw pleasure of his probing touch.

She felt panic then. Her body was being pushed to the very edge of something she could only dimly perceive, and the instinctive drives demanded she reach that mysterious place no matter what effort it took or what cost it demanded. Tension wound so tightly, she thought she would shatter from it. The inferno inside her burned out of control, the most exquisitely sensitive nerves in her body responding to his stroking fingers, and she was carried along on a rushing wave of sensation that was suddenly frightening.

"Max?" Her voice seemed to come from a stranger, thin and ragged, and the panic inside her was gripping her as strongly as the desperate striving she could feel in every taut muscle of her body.

"Don't fight it, sweetheart," he muttered against her flesh, the vibrations of his rough words a new caress. "Feel . . . let yourself feel. . . ."

Dinah hadn't realized she was fighting, but his low words made her abruptly aware of a small, wary part of her that *was* trying to hold back. Giving herself over totally to pleasure was a new experience—and a terrifying one. It was so utterly uncontrollable, as if she were being asked to fling herself over a cliff and trust him to catch her.

Trust . . . A different kind of trust from what he had already won from her. A kind of trust she had never given to anyone because it had never been asked of her. Until now. She had to let go, to willingly give up control of her rational mind and make herself completely defenseless—physically as well as emotionally. To lose herself in him until her very identity drowned in sensation, to give up all that she was.

In that brief, stark moment, Dinah finally understood. The vulnerability she had feared with Max had little to do with memories of rape. Only the act itself could be forced, the physical submission; the mental and emotional surrender was something that could never be taken from her, it was something she had to offer up willingly. And her mind resisted the compulsion to give in to Max now because she knew that capitulation was the ultimate one.

It was never the nightmare of pain and force she had feared, it was the surrender to pleasure.

Dinah realized that, absorbing the shock even as her body quivered at the precipice he had brought her to. The panicked desperation of her body for release fought the equally panicked resistance of her mind to that starkly intimate, ultimate surrender. Then Max lifted his head to look at her, his compelling eyes so fiercely tender that they broke her resistance. And her heart.

"Dinah," he whispered. "Please, darling, trust me."

A soft, wordless cry winged free of her, and Dinah willingly let herself go. She let the rushing wave carry her, a wild rapture filling her at the sheer freedom of it. Her body shuddered, then every aching muscle tensed. It seemed to last an eternity, a breathless, yearning, burning eternity, and then her senses shattered in the most incredible pleasure she could have imagined. Her entire body was gripped by a pulsing ecstasy, and her astonished, exultant cry of release was lost in Max's mouth.

In the stunned aftermath, Dinah could only lie trembling, conscious of her pounding heart and gasping breath, of the faint throbbing inside her. She hadn't known . . . hadn't even suspected it would be like that. So incredible. So overwhelming. She felt the bed shift, and turned her head to watch dazedly as Max swiftly removed the remainder of his clothing. In the lamplight, his powerful body was magnificent. She hadn't known he would be so beautiful, or that the sight of him could stir her numbed senses anew.

Her emotional surrender had brought Dinah a kind of serenity she hadn't even realized was lacking in her, as well as the first joyous bloom of her sexuality. Those petals unfurled now, rich with the varied colors of desire and a wonderful new knowledge of pleasure. He was beautiful, and she wanted him.

His need was overwhelmingly obvious in the swollen fullness of his manhood, and Dinah might have felt fear then if the bonds of trust were uncertain. But they were strong. And what she saw when she looked at him brought only wonder and desire. The stark physical power of size and muscle, the raw virility and sheer force of passion, the burning tenderness in his eyes, all intensified her hunger for him.

If she felt any nervousness, it was only in her ability to give him the same ecstasy he had given her.

Max came down beside her on the bed, his body so hard and burning with the feverish need in him that it ignited her own smoldering passion. His mouth took hers hungrily, his hands stroking her heated flesh, and Dinah felt the sweet, maddening tension winding inside her again. Her trembling fingers stroked his chest and shoulders, his back, while her body responded wildly, helplessly, to his touch.

"I want to please you."

Her soft, breathless statement nearly broke the tattered remains of Max's control. Please him? Dear God, he was half out of his mind with pleasure now. He hadn't dared to hope she would be able to respond to him so freely, and the simple fact that she had—especially after the endless moment when she'd resisted—had been a delight beyond measure. And even though delaying his own release had been pure torment, caressing her silky flesh had given him a more intense pleasure than he'd ever known while driving his desire for her higher and higher.

"You are," he muttered against her throat, feeling the hoarse rumble of his own words. "You do." An incredible wave of love and need swept over him, the emotions so acute that he wanted to merge his very cells with hers, join with her so completely that they could never be separated in this life or any other.

She was touching him eagerly, her soft hands making his body shudder, and he was so near the edge, he thought he really had gone mad. Groaning, he struggled to hang on to the last fiber of control as he eased her legs apart and rose above her. Even in his urgency, a watchful part of his awareness was fixed totally on her face, alert for any sign of fear or panic. She was looking up at him, her beautiful eyes dazed and so dark, they were nearly black, and when her arms slid up around his neck he knew there wouldn't be any fear.

Still, he was as careful as his rigid body and critical need allowed, easing into her tight heat very slowly. Her breath caught, and for an instant she seemed to tense, but it was with surprise and wonder rather than panic. Her body admitted him willingly, sheathed him with a slick, silky welcome that jerked a groan of fierce pleasure from his tight throat.

Dinah couldn't believe the sensations. So incredibly intimate, so shatteringly sweet. She could feel him sinking deeply inside her, pulsing, feel her body stretching to receive an alien yet instinctively familiar presence. There was pressure and fullness, and for an instant she couldn't breathe, all her awareness focused totally on the merging of her body with his. His weight eased down, covering her, and though a part of her was starkly aware of how defenseless a woman was—*she* was—in the act of possession, what she felt most was a profound feeling of satisfaction.

The satisfaction was in joining, but the joining wasn't complete and her body knew it. The sensual tension he had built in her demanded more. She lifted her hips a little to take more of him, but that just made the burning ache inside her increase until she couldn't bear it.

"Max," she whispered raggedly, her arms tight around his neck and her legs lifting to cradle his body. "Max, please—"

His mouth covered hers, taking the plea, and he began to move. He was slow and careful at first, giving Dinah time to absorb the sensations. He didn't lose control; she took it from him. Her body caught the rhythm of lovemaking, and her lithe movements beneath him were a seduction he couldn't resist.

The strain of holding himself back for so long had become an intolerable necessity, and for the first time in his life he felt the primitive inside himself, the ancient, blind instincts and compulsive urgency that drove a male to mate with his chosen female. It was a dance, a battle, a mutual possession so intense that the culmination of it was a vast, soul-consuming rapture.

For a long time, Dinah felt almost disconnected from her body. Her mind floated, a lingering astonishment and awe filling her consciousness. Nobody had told her it could be like that. She knew she had never been closer to another human being, and if it was an experience granted only rarely, she was deeply grateful it had been granted to her.

Gradually, she became aware of sensations. Her

body was limp, sated in a wonderful exhaustion. There were faint aftershocks deep inside her, the final, gentle ripples of pleasure. And the blissfully hard, heavy weight of his body pressing her into the bed was surprisingly both comfortable and satisfying. He was still with her, still inside her, and her body didn't want to give him up even for a moment. She murmured a faint protest when Max pushed himself up on his elbows, her arms tightening around his neck, and her lips clung to his when he kissed her tenderly.

In the lamplight, his face was still hard, but she wasn't disturbed or deceived by the mask nature had given him. His eyes were warm and soft, and she knew that although this very large man might appear to be made of pure granite, he had a gentle heart she trusted implicitly.

"I love you," he murmured. "God, Dinah, I love you so much."

Dinah didn't even think about her response, because the utter truth came without the need of thought. "I'm glad. Because I love you too."

Max half closed his eyes and swallowed hard. Huskily, he said, "I hope you're sure, sweetheart. If I lost you now, it would kill me."

She stroked his lean cheek with trembling fingers, the happiness inside her so great, she wondered why she didn't burst from it. "Oh, Max . . . I think I loved you from the beginning, from that first night in the museum when you came out of nowhere to save me. I was just too afraid to admit it. Too afraid of—of giving."

"I know." He kissed her softly, a fleeting pain in his eyes. Pain for her. "Someone took too much from you once, and you didn't want to give anything else."

It didn't surprise her that he understood; Max would always understand. It was one of the reasons she loved him.

"I want to give to you," she told him. "I want to give you everything."

"You have." He kissed her again, more deeply this time, and Dinah could feel the slow renewal of need in him as well as in herself.

Max lifted his head, a rough sound escaping him. His face tightened, and his eyes were becoming hooded with that sensual look she loved so much. "If I don't stop now . . ." he said somewhat thickly.

Dinah held him with her arms, and her thighs tightened on his hips. "Don't stop," she whispered, raising her head off the pillow to kiss him hungrily, her tongue probing with a new and sensuous skill.

For a moment, Max tried to be sensible, worried that the demands of passion—hers and his—would take too great a toll on her slight body. But then her inner muscles clenched around him, sending hot, intense pleasure through every nerve he possessed, and rationality scattered. His body compulsively pressed even deeper within her, and a tortured groan rumbled up from his chest.

It didn't occur to Dinah that the cost of this fierce passion would be sore muscles, and if it had she wouldn't have cared. She wanted to give him everything she had and take everything he would give her. Loving him was all that mattered to her.

This time, their loving was quick, almost wild, both of them hungry for sensation and completion. She wouldn't let him be gentle even though he tried, stealing his control as surely as she'd stolen his heart, and her response was so sweetly passionate, he couldn't temper the force of his own need. She matched him on every level, giving and unafraid, and they rushed to the precipice, and over, together.

Afterward, they shared a hot shower, and Dinah dried her hair while Max raided the kitchen. It was nearly two in the morning by the time the snack was consumed and they lay together once again in the wide bed. Since the weekend was ahead with its promise of laziness, and since neither was sleepy anyway, the lamp remained on and they talked quietly.

At some point, Dinah finally recalled the visitor of hours before, and lifted her head from Max's shoulder. Her speculation had been pushed aside by more important matters, but now she could think with some semblance of rationality.

"Who is Keane Tyler?" she asked.

With his eyes mostly closed and his body obviously in a state of total relaxation, Max murmured, "You met him tonight."

"I was *introduced* to him tonight," Dinah corrected a bit wryly. "I actually met him after lunch. He was the driver you sent with Morgan and me on the shopping trip."

Gray eyes gleamed at her as Max roused himself. "Oh, you noticed that."

Dinah folded her hands on his broad chest and rested her chin on them. "Perceptive of me, I know. Who is he, Max?"

Max had one arm around her, his fingers toying with her silky copper hair, while his other hand stroked her side in a gentle, lazy motion. He paused for a moment before answering, not so much with hesitation, she thought, but as if he were debating silently. Then he sighed.

"Inspector Keane Tyler."

That, she hadn't expected. She raised her head and frowned slightly. "Police?"

"San Francisco's finest. He's also a very good friend, sweetheart. And since he's not very fond of criminals—especially those who use innocent victims as tools—he's doing what he can to help. Even if that means driving a limo to keep an eye on you."

After a moment, Dinah nodded slowly. "I see. He's your contact with the police. When you got those reports on me from Boston—?"

"Keane's the one who provided access to the

records, yes. He's also been checking police files trying to come up with suspects. Thieves who pressure or blackmail insiders into helping them get what they're after."

Dinah made herself ask, even though a part of her wanted to avoid knowing. She was determined not to hide from anything even inside the "safe place" Max had provided for her. "Has he found anyone who works that way?"

With a small grimace, Max said, "Quite a few, sad to say. He's eliminated most of them for various reasons, leaving only one he thinks could be our man. That's why he came here tonight, to tell me what he'd found. But . . . he refused to give me the man's name."

"Why?"

Max continued to toy with her hair, winding the bright strands around his fingers. For the first time, he avoided her gaze, and his voice was evasive. "Cops don't like pointing fingers without evidence."

Dinah was puzzled, as much by his tone as the words. "But if he was only looking for suspects, why wouldn't he tell you what he'd found? Why come all the way up here to tell you he *couldn't* tell you anything?"

Clearing his throat, Max said, "Well, the problem is that the suspect's out of our reach—at least for now. Since he whispered, you wouldn't be able to positively identify his voice, and we have no evidence it was him. We can't prove he's done anything. And, since he's never been convicted of a crime, Keane can't even legitimately pull him in for questioning."

All that made sense, but Dinah was still certain there was more than Max was telling her. "All right, but why wouldn't Keane give you a name?"

"He thinks I might recognize it."

Dinah waited, looking at him gravely, and after another moment Max sighed and met her gaze.

"He also thinks that if I knew the man's name, I

might be tempted to . . . take matters into my own hands."

"Would you?" she asked quietly.

"Yes."

It didn't really surprise Dinah. She didn't have to be told that Max respected the law. She also didn't have to be told that powerful men tended to be quick to use their influence in order to protect loved ones.

"Fighting my battles?" she murmured.

"I wish I could." Max smiled slightly, and his hand slid underneath the silky weight of her hair to stroke her neck. Her skin was soft and warm, and his voice roughened when he said, "I wish I could protect you from anything that could harm you. I love you, Dinah."

She touched his hard cheek, and a wavering smile curved her lips. "I love you too, Max. I think they call that giving hostages to fortune—and nobody ever said fortune was safe, any more than life is. You can't protect me, not from everything bad. I know that. You know it."

He did—but the knowing didn't make it easier to accept.

Dinah was still smiling. "You're my hostage in fortune's hands, remember. Whatever happens to you affects me—and you're a much more likely target for danger because of who and what you are. I have to live with that, Max, just like you have to live with the fact that you can't protect me from life. If we don't take the risk, we can't love."

He knew she was right. Even more, he could see the strength that was being reborn in her, as fragile as a seedling but putting down roots that would anchor her against even the fiercest wind. She was healing. Even with all that had happened to her, with everything that had been taken away from her, she was willing to risk her heart.

For him.

"Some risks," Max murmured huskily, "are worth

taking. I learned that a long time ago." He lifted his head to kiss her deeply, his hands beginning to wander with more than just lazy enjoyment.

Dinah made a little sound of pleasure and kissed him with matching hunger.

"I can't get enough of you," he said as he shifted position, easing her onto her back and rising on an elbow beside her.

She wreathed her arms around his neck, her desire for him growing as if she hadn't felt utterly sated only a short time ago. "Good," she whispered, and lifted her mouth to his.

Mrs. Perry took due note of the changes when they emerged from Max's bedroom late in the morning. She had brunch ready for them, and merely commented that there was plenty of food in the freezer, and that since they obviously no longer required a chaperon she would revert to being a daily housekeeper instead of a live-in. The announcement was made briskly, giving neither of them an opportunity to question or comment, and Max chuckled when they were alone again in the dining room.

"I had a feeling she'd do that."

A bit guiltily, Dinah said, "She certainly seems to be in a hurry to leave. Did she turn her life upside down to stay here at night for my sake?"

"No." Max grinned at her. "For mine. And that's why she's in a hurry to leave—so we can be alone. She's been after me for fifteen years to settle down, and the day I first brought you here she knew you were my last hope."

Dinah made a somewhat comical sound of disbelief. "Last hope? From what I've heard, half the women in San Francisco have been after you."

Max eyed her. "Morgan talks too much."

"That's beside the point." Dinah kept her expression severe. "The truth is—"

"The truth," he interrupted firmly, "is that I've had a very normal sex life for a man of my age, with a reasonable number of relationships which I consider pleasant—and past. In my defense, let me remind you that when you were twelve, I was twenty-four."

Dinah sniffed, enjoying the teasing. "So you've had all these years to sow your wild oats?"

"I was never wild," he protested, his gray eyes gleaming at her.

"No, rumor has it you've been very discreet," she said in bland agreement. "At least in San Francisco. I expect that means you have mistresses scattered up and down the West Coast."

"Don't be ridiculous." He paused, sipping his coffee, then added, "Only across the Bay."

"Well, get rid of them."

Max frowned at her. "That's a bit cruel, don't you think? After all, it isn't their fault I took one look at you and lost interest in every other woman." When she remained unrelenting, he sighed mournfully. "Very well, consider it done. My heart wasn't really in it any longer, to be honest. Funny thing. Somebody stole it."

"Your heart?"

"Snatched it away without any warning at all. It's gone for good too."

"You're a very disarming man," she said with a note of reproach.

He chuckled suddenly and lifted one of her hands to his lips briefly. "Are you really jealous? I mean, is my past something we'd better talk about seriously?"

"No," she said a bit wryly, "I can hardly feel jealous about women who knew you before I did. That wouldn't be reasonable."

His lips curved in a smile. "True."

Dinah cleared her throat. "However, I'll admit to feeling a little curious about one woman."

Max didn't exactly wince, but it was obvious he knew the answer when he asked, "And that is?"

"Nyssa Armstrong," Dinah murmured.

He was silent for a moment, looking at her very seriously, his hand still holding hers. Then, slowly, he said, "What Morgan said about Nyssa is pretty much true—but not really very amusing. I've known her for years, and I've watched her go from one man to another, always coming away with some trinket she wanted. And, year by year, she's gotten even more . . . desperately hungry, as if she's empty of some vital thing she needs. I knew I couldn't help her, and I wasn't about to help her go on destroying herself. I never slept with her, Dinah."

How many men, Dinah wondered dimly, would turn away from a stunningly beautiful, seductive blonde because he knew a brief affair with him would be destructive to her? A few, perhaps, but not many.

She didn't realize she had moved toward him until Max pushed his chair back slightly and she was in his lap with her face buried against his neck. "I love you," she murmured.

His arms went around her, hard yet gentle. "I love you too, sweetheart. More than I'll ever be able to tell you."

Eight

They spent the remainder of the weekend alone in the apartment, taking little notice of the world outside. As Mrs. Perry had said, there was plenty of food in the freezer, and Max turned on his answering machine, closed his study door, and unplugged the extension in his bedroom so they wouldn't be disturbed by the various business calls he normally got during a weekend.

"What if there's an emergency?" Dinah asked idly.

"Then whoever it is can come here, and the security guard downstairs will buzz," he answered, supremely indifferent to emergencies.

There was, apparently, no emergency, nor any friend or business associate desperate enough to come to the building and plead with the guard in the lobby. In any case, they were left undisturbed.

They had been living together for a week, but Dinah discovered very quickly that there was a great deal more than quiet companionship between lovers. Especially when love was newly found and desire never cooled to less than smoldering embers. She and Max couldn't be together without touching, and even the most casual touch between them was like dry wood tossed on the glowing embers.

She also discovered that her emotional surrender had indeed been complete; love and desire, once admitted and consummated, became as much a part of her as her beating heart. And it changed her. It changed everything. She felt like a different person, stronger, surer, happier with herself, and more in control of her own life. She had gone from being a woman with shattered trust to a woman whose trust—in Max—was absolute.

His touch was so healing, it was incredible.

"Why didn't you tell me this would happen?" Dinah murmured late Saturday afternoon. They were lying together before a crackling fire in the marble fireplace, thick carpet and cushions from the couch making a comfortable place. They had begun a chess game about an hour before, but the board on the coffee table still held all the pieces except for a couple of pawns. The game hadn't lasted long before both of them had become distracted, as always, by each other.

For once, Max deliberately chose to ignore the real meaning of her question, and answered solemnly. "How could I possibly know you'd be so sexy sitting on the floor wearing nothing but my shirt that I'd go crazy?"

"Max . . ."

"I couldn't even wait to take you to bed. Or even get to the couch. But I plead extenuating circumstances. Here I am trying to be a sensitive lover and not overwhelm you by lunging at you every couple of hours, and you keep encouraging me by responding so wonderfully, I can barely think of anything else. I refuse to take the blame. It's all your fault for telling me gravely that sore muscles need to be exercised. You told me that this morning, too, and I went crazy then. By Monday, neither of us will be able to walk without help."

Dinah raised herself on an elbow to look down at him, her hand beginning to wander exploringly over his broad chest. She slid her fingers into the thick, springy mat of hair, pausing when she felt the tight point of his nipple.

He opened his eyes to look at her and said, "Or maybe by tomorrow."

"You didn't answer my question," she murmured, the tip of one finger circling his nipple slowly.

"Keep doing that, and I won't be able to say anything that makes sense," he warned, after clearing his throat.

Dinah smiled, but continued the little caress. "What have you done to me?" she wondered in a marveling voice. "I feel so different. I hear myself saying things I could never imagine myself saying, watch myself doing things that seem impossible for me. And it all feels so perfect. So familiar."

He reached up to brush a strand of hair away from her face, then slid his hand under the warm mass to stroke the sensitive nape of her neck. "If I did that, I'm glad," he said. "But it wasn't only me, Dinah. You were always meant to be a warm, loving woman. I knew that the moment I first saw you."

"Is that why you gave me a safe place? So I could know it too?"

Slowly, he said, "You were scared and hurting, and I couldn't bear that. I knew you were capable of love, I didn't know if you could love me. I was afraid I'd push too hard, ask too much of you before you were ready, but I had to be near you, had to hope you could learn to trust me enough. I love you, sweetheart. That's the only true answer to the *why* of everything. Because I love you."

She looked at him for a long moment, her lips curving in the beautiful, sweet smile that never failed to stop his heart. "That's my answer too. Why I feel so different, why everything is perfect. Because I love you."

She moved before he could, her head lowering so that her lips could explore his throat, his chest. Her hand was still caressing him as well, and his body responded, as always, with such sudden intensity, it was almost like a blow. He wanted her so much, it was like madness.

Was madness.

It was almost impossible for him to remain still, but the intense pleasure of her touch more than made up for the strain of holding himself rigid, and he wasn't about to complain as she caressed him. It was a sweet torture like nothing he'd ever felt before. It was wonderful.

Max always had believed there was a warm and loving woman inside Dinah, hidden at the wounded, wary core of her. But he hadn't dared to hope that that woman would emerge so completely and confidently. So he was doubly delighted now when she began loving him, encouraging her with soft touches and murmurs of his own.

What she lacked in experience, she more than made up for in simple eagerness, exploring his body with a loving hunger more inflaming than he would have thought possible. It became more and more difficult for him to lie still until it was sheer torture, until his body punished him for his patience, every raw nerve screaming with a blazing desire for more than her touch. His muscles tightened and quivered in a blind response he could barely control, and a primal sound he wasn't even aware of making rumbled deep in his chest.

As always, she snapped the threads of his control, leaving him so desperate for her that his awareness of everything in the world except her and his desire for her vanished. Groaning, he lifted her over him, merging their bodies in a single strong motion. The flickering firelight was alive in her glimmering eyes as she looked down at him, and her glorious hair tumbled wildly about her shoulders as she instinctively began to move in a lithe, lazy seduction.

The torment of her touch became an even sweeter

agony that drove him. His body was so rigid, every muscle ached, and all his straining senses were filled with the exquisite sensations of her body clasping his. He took it as long as he could, but finally he surged beneath her, his big hands on her hips controlling, insisting the teasing was past.

His urgency ignited her own, and Dinah could feel herself carried along on that incredible wave, her frantic body joining his in a headlong rush toward release. And even as ecstasy shuddered through her, even as she collapsed on his heaving chest in a profound satisfaction, she was murmuring over and over that she loved him.

He had been right. That *was* the why of everything.

Max didn't check his answering machine until early Monday morning just after breakfast and before they were ready to leave for the museum, and then only because she reminded him to. Dinah was shrugging into her coat in the living room when he emerged from his study, and though his hard face was expressionless, she knew something was wrong.

"What is it?" she asked immediately.

"Nothing imperative," he reassured her. "Just a bit troubling. There were messages from Morgan and Wolfe, left sometime yesterday. The security company we're using at the museum fired one of their employees Saturday, and she's being questioned by the police."

"Why?"

"Apparently, her supervisor caught her trying to break into restricted files containing security setups for some of their clients."

"The museum?" Dinah said quickly.

Max shrugged into his coat. "I don't know. Wolfe's message said he'd have all the information by this morning, and that he'd be at the museum early so we can discuss the situation. We'll find out when we get there."

Dinah didn't say anything more until they were in the car and heading toward the museum. After the wonderful, extremely intimate weekend with Max, she was a bit jarred by the reminder of unpleasant possibilities surrounding the museum and Max's exhibit. At the same time, she was able to view those possibilities much more clearly than she'd been able to before.

"Max?"

"What is it, love?" He was holding her hand on his thigh, and turned his head briefly to give her a smile.

"That suspect Keane Tyler found . . . There's no way to get him without some kind of lure, is there?"

Max's fingers tightened around hers. "We'll find a way."

"I don't think so," she said quietly. "Not without me."

"I won't risk you," Max said immediately.

All her instincts told Dinah she was ready to fight and, even more, that she needed to. It was a kind of healing as important to her as the now painless scars from the hurt two years ago. Whatever it took, whatever she had to do, Dinah knew she couldn't run—or hide—anymore.

After a moment, she said, "Does Wolfe know about me?"

Max knew what she was asking, though the abrupt change of subject surprised him, and after a quick glance at her he answered honestly. "Yes. Since he's heading security, and since he'd found the holes in your background when he ran a security check, I had to tell him the truth."

That was understandable, and Dinah nodded slightly. She herself had confided in Morgan during their shopping trip—when no one could overhear them—because she'd known Max wouldn't tell her and because Dinah felt the director of the exhibit had a right to know of the threat. Morgan's empathic pain and sympathy had been instant and genuine, her support absolute, and Dinah felt no regrets in having revealed her past to the other woman.

"Does Wolfe know your friend Keane found a suspect?" she asked Max, trying mentally to figure out who knew what. She had the odd feeling that sharing information with the wrong person could upset some plan of Max's, although there was nothing on which to base her feelings except intuition.

"No, I haven't had a chance to tell him. Why?"

Dinah hesitated, then spoke slowly. "I don't know. Something's bothering me about all this. I can't make it come clear in my mind. Maybe when we find out what happened with the security company I'll figure it out."

"Dinah . . ."

She smiled. "I don't mean to sound so vague, Max, it's just that I really don't know what's bothering me. There's a . . . wrongness somewhere in all this. I didn't notice anything before, maybe because I was just too scared to see the whole picture clearly, but when you told me about Wolfe's message a bell went off in my head."

Max frowned slightly. "The whole picture?"

"Yes." Dinah tried to concentrate. "The thief trying to use me . . . I have a feeling we've all missed something."

Max looked at her again, but didn't ask any more questions. Until they had whatever information Wolfe could provide, even questions would be mere conjecture.

"The security company's keeping it as quiet as possible," Wolfe said, "for obvious reasons. They had no choice but to notify clients who might find their security systems vulnerable now. I got the call Saturday afternoon, and I sat in yesterday when the police questioned the woman."

"She was forced to do it?" Max asked quietly.

They were back in their makeshift conference area in the storage room. As before, Max, Dinah, Morgan, and Wolfe were present. The normally laconic Wolfe had quite a bit to say today, though he still didn't waste words.

"According to her statement, yes. However, her situation's a bit different from Dinah's: She was being blackmailed. It seems that about three years ago, she was working at another security company somewhere in the Midwest. She made good use of her job to get information for a boyfriend, who subsequently robbed a jewelry store. He was caught, and he fingered her—but she was gone. She changed her name and, God knows how, managed to get another job with our security company. When the blackmailer got in touch, he knew all about her past deeds, and reminded her she was looking at an accessory charge."

A bit wryly, Morgan said, "Am I alone in thinking maybe we should change security companies? After that technician of theirs blew the hard disk on Friday—"

Max looked at her. "After he did what?"

It was Wolfe who answered, and with a perfect poker face. "We would have told you at the party Friday night, but you appeared to have other things on your mind. And after that, nobody could get in touch with you."

Max glanced at Dinah, a gleam in his eyes, but said merely, "I see. So—what did the technician do?"

"He blew the hard disk," Morgan reported succinctly. "Wrecked weeks of work and we'll have to replace the disk—which won't be cheap, but the company *insists* on footing the bill. You should have heard Wolfe when he called them up to, um, report the situation. He used words I'll swear were completely original," she finished in simple admiration.

"I was upset," the security expert said mildly. "I wanted them to know I was upset."

"Which they undoubtedly do," Morgan murmured. "Along with me, all the night guards, and the last half-dozen museum visitors on Friday—who couldn't wait to get out of here when they heard all the roaring."

"Very funny," Wolfe told her

Morgan grinned, then went back to her original question. "But the point is—can we stay with them?"

Wolfe shrugged. "They're supposed to be the best, in spite of their very red faces at the moment. And their CEO called me about half an hour ago swearing on all he holds dear that there won't be another screwup. He's even pulling their top computer specialist off a job in Europe to take over for the kid who made a royal mess of things Friday. The replacement should be here within two weeks."

After thinking it over, Max shook his head. "I say we stick with the devil we know. They'll be a lot more careful now than any new company coming in."

"You're the boss," Morgan murmured, quite obviously keeping doubts to herself.

With that matter settled, Wolfe went on. "It struck me that having someone inside this museum *and* inside the security company we happen to be using targeted by an apparent thief was a bit too much of a coincidence. I thought there was a good chance it was the same man. It made sense that once his string to Dinah was cut, he'd look for another way in. The security company was a logical choice."

"Did she see him?" Dinah asked.

"No, but she thinks she'll recognize his voice. Maybe enough to identify him in a lineup—maybe not. She wants to be helpful, though, and helping the police now is a sensible idea. Anyway, it was the beginning of last week when he called and leaned on her. What he wanted, she says, was very specific."

"Our security layout?" Morgan asked.

Wolfe smiled. "No—and the museum wasn't mentioned except in a group with an art gallery and a jewelry store. He named the three places, wanted to know which had computerized systems not yet on-line, and if any one did, when the scheduled completion date was. She reported to him that the museum was the only one, and gave him the date our system was scheduled to go on-line. It was when he called her Saturday that he wanted the total security layout. Of the museum."

Slowly, Max said, "According to the original specifications, we should have been on-line—when? Morgan?"

"By this coming Friday," she said definitely. "The technician set us back weeks with his mistakes, but we'd already revised the original deadline anyway for other reasons. But *that* wouldn't have been in the company's files. All they keep are the original specifications, and a final date of when the system actually goes on-line."

"So as far as he knows," Dinah realized, "the system here goes on-line Friday."

"But what good does that do him?" Morgan wanted to know, frowning. "The collection won't be brought here until the system's on-line, no matter when that is."

"That's it," Dinah said suddenly, quietly. She looked at Max. "That was what was bothering me. From the beginning, he was moving too fast, applying too much pressure on me—*if* his target wouldn't be here for weeks."

"Exactly," Wolfe said.

Max was still gazing at Dinah, nodding slightly as he realized. "The collection wasn't his target."

Ruefully, Wolfe said, "The first thing any good detective will tell you is—never assume. All of us assumed he was after the collection, even though we're sitting on a museum *already* filled with very valuable items, most of which would be a hell of a lot easier to fence. It always bugged me that he moved on Dinah as early as he did, but I couldn't figure out what my common sense was trying to tell me."

"Neither could I," Dinah murmured.

Slowly, looking at Wolfe again, Max said, "The collection won't be here for weeks, and everyone knows you don't play a trump card until it'll do you the most good. A hold based on fear is very fragile. He couldn't be stupid enough to believe he could go on on terrorizing Dinah and keeping her under his control for weeks. It just isn't smart."

Almost to herself, Dinah said, "He wanted me to tell him what was in the wing where the exhibit's being set up. That's why Max found me coming out of there that night."

Wolfe nodded. "My guess is that he didn't want to waste his time in a wing where there was nothing of value."

"All right," Max said, "so far, it sounds good to me. Especially given his concern with when the security system would go on-line. The best possible time to hit this museum would be in the last few days before the new system is activated."

Grimly, Wolfe said, "The whole building's vulnerable then. The coded locks on each door are the only previous security measure that would still be operating that last day or two: Lasers, motion sensors, and pressure plates are all dead until the changeover. If he can get in, and avoid the guards—which we all know is simple given the size of the place—then any thief worth his salt could bypass the individual alarms on the display cases and walk out of here a very rich man."

Morgan was looking disgusted, probably at herself for having assumed, but she said, "Would he dare now? He's tried to use two people and lost them both. With his latest victim in the hands of the police—"

"The police are betting he doesn't know that, and I agree." Wolfe's voice was certain. "She was supposed to meet him Saturday night, and give him a computer diskette with the entire security layout— the *current* layout—of the museum. She was caught late in the morning, and taken out of the building through a very secure rear entrance in the company of two plainclothes cops. Within a couple of hours, the cops arranged to quietly and quickly empty her apartment to make it look like she ran. A very natural thing for her to do."

"So he still may try," Max said.

"I think he will," Wolfe agreed. "He's gone too far to let go now, and as far as he knows nobody can connect him to the museum or the security company. Besides, if he's who I think he is, one thing he doesn't do is give up easily."

"Who do you think he is?"

In an offhand tone, Wolfe said, "I took a chance and asked a contact with Interpol for a list of thieves with his M.O. who could be in the San Francisco area."

Dinah very carefully didn't look at Max, and hoped she didn't react in any way. It was up to Max whether he chose to tell Wolfe he already knew there was a good suspect. Dinah had a feeling he wouldn't—and she was pretty sure she knew why he would feign ignorance.

Max's voice was calm, giving nothing away. "And you ended up with one name?"

"Yeah. Unfortunately, there isn't much on him to justify an arrest, or even a search warrant. The police here in the city would love to move on him— but he has to move first."

"Who is he?" Max asked.

In an almost comically careful tone, Wolfe said, "I'd rather not say. All I have is a suspicion he's our man—not a certainty. I know you, Max, and I have a fairly good idea of how you feel about this guy. Sorry, but I'd rather not have to explain to Mother if you ended up in jail."

Max stared at him somewhat grimly, but there was a reluctant flicker of amusement in his eyes. Dinah thought he probably wanted to comment on the fact that Wolfe was the second man intent on saving him from the consequences of reckless action, but since no mention had been made of Keane he was unable to.

Finally, in a mild tone, he said, "I *can* generally control myself, you know."

"I know. Generally."

Reluctantly admitting defeat, Max said, "All right, so how does your *suspicion* of who he is help us?"

"Well, after what happened with the security company, I talked to a friend of yours in the San Francisco P.D. You have good friends, Max—Keane Tyler has been very helpful."

"Good," Max murmured.

Dinah had a peculiar impulse to laugh, but conquered it. Max was up to something, she thought. He wasn't exactly lying to Wolfe, but he certainly wasn't volunteering information. She made a mental note to pin him down later, when they were alone, and find out just what was going on.

Wolfe seemed unaware of his brother's possible duplicity, and went on calmly. "Thanks to Keane, the police have our blackmailer-thief's phone tapped and him under constant surveillance. They were willing to overlook the lack of evidence just on the possibility they could get their hands on at least one of the thieves in the city—especially since that gang's eluded them, and the mayor's screaming for an arrest." Wolfe shook his head. "So, anyway, if he doesn't move by Friday, then we have no way of guessing when it will be. But I think he'll move in the next few days."

"He doesn't have a way in," Max said in a voice that was suddenly flat.

Dinah knew there was only one answer—just as Max knew. She also knew he hated it, and would do everything he could to convince her there was some other way. Even if there wasn't.

Quietly, she said, "Yes, he has a way in. Me. I'm the only one left who can open a door for him. If he wants in, he'll have to contact me before Friday."

Max shook his head just once.

Wolfe looked from him to Dinah, his face expressionless. His voice still calm, he said, "After the incident with the open door, we fixed it so the doors can't be left unlocked. If you did unlock one, you'd have to be there—holding it open for him."

Dinah felt herself shiver, and then got angry at herself because Max looked at her just then and she knew he'd seen it. She didn't want to make this any harder on him than necessary, so she fought to hide her stab of fear.

Softly, he said, "I won't risk you."

She met his gaze—and couldn't break the contact. Vaguely, she was aware of Wolfe speaking, and then Morgan.

"I think I'll get a cup of coffee."

"I think I'll join you."

Was it that visible, Dinah wondered dimly, this strange, intense connection between them? She had a feeling it was, that the other two had seen it and had left simply because they recognized an intimacy that demanded privacy.

When they were alone, Dinah said quietly, "You told me that some risks are worth taking."

"Nothing's worth risking you. Nothing."

She hesitated. "Max, you told me something else too. We all need a safe place where we can heal, where we can get strong enough to fight. You gave me that, and I'll always be grateful. But I can't turn what you gave me into a cage. If I don't do what I can to make that bastard pay for what he did to me, then I really will be hiding with you. And neither of us could live with that for very long."

Even though Max's face didn't change, she could feel the struggle going on inside him. It was his nature to do all he could to protect those he loved, and fighting one's own nature could be a terrible battle.

Finally, a bit hoarsely, Max said, "He may not call. He may just give up and pick another target."

She nodded. "But if he does, I have to convince him he still controls me. I have to open the door for him."

Max rose and pulled her up into his arms, holding her tightly. It was the first thing she had asked of him, and he couldn't refuse. As much as he wanted to. It was another thing he'd learned about risks.

Sometimes *taking* a risk was more important than the risk itself.

They all agreed the thief would most likely try to reach her at the museum. The apartment number was unlisted and known to only a handful of people, and, besides, it would be a bit rash of the man to deliberately upset Dinah—which a call would certainly do—with Max within earshot. It took the combined arguments of both Wolfe and Dinah to persuade Max not to remain at the museum during the entire day just so she *would* be alone in her office for several hours at a stretch, but he finally agreed.

He didn't like it, but he agreed, then made very sure Dinah was protected by a guard at the end of the hallway of offices as well as by Wolfe's presence in the museum.

Nothing happened on Monday or Tuesday, except that they were all tense and restless. Max and Dinah returned to his apartment each evening, and both of them made the most of the hours they had alone together. As time passed, Dinah became even more certain that there was more to Max's decision to exhibit his collection than he'd told her. She waited until Tuesday night, when he was in a condition best described as defenseless and at her mercy, to demand an answer. However, Max was a strong man even in that state, and managed—albeit in a growl—to say that he'd tell her all his secrets on their honeymoon.

Dinah accepted that, mostly because Max wasn't really defenseless at all, as it turned out. And if he was at her mercy, she was also quite definitely at his. Within seconds of his answer, she not only was untroubled by what he hadn't told her, but had entirely lost interest in the subject.

For the first time since she had come to stay with Max, Dinah was awakened just before dawn by a nightmare. She awoke abruptly, a cry locked in her throat, to find herself safe in Max's arms. He was sleeping deeply, and she was very careful not to disturb him as she slipped from the bed.

She found her nightgown—it was lying over a chair where it had been flung earlier—she put it on, then eased out of the bedroom without turning on a light. The apartment wasn't completely dark, and by the time she reached the windows in the living room the sunrise had painted the sky with swirls of purple and pink.

Dinah stood gazing out, watching dawn arrive, remembering her nightmare. Not the old nightmare, but another one created by and equally sick mind. A mind that could coldly conceive of and execute a campaign of terror—out of greed.

From the instant Max had told her he believed the man here wasn't the man who had raped her in Boston, Dinah hadn't wanted to think about it very much. It had, somehow, seemed less terrible to believe there was only one man, even though it had terrified her to think he had followed her across a country after two years. One inhuman man was enough for any woman to encounter in her lifetime . . . and lightning never struck the same place twice, they said.

Except that they were wrong. Lightning had been known to strike the same place twice. There were people who'd been struck more than once. And, wishful thinking aside, there was far more than one brutal man in the world.

Her mind had shied away from the idea that she could have been used twice by different men bent on satisfying their own vicious needs. But now, for the first time, Dinah accepted that as the cold truth.

And what she felt as she stood there gazing out on the dawn wasn't pain—it was anger. Bad enough she'd been attacked once, her life changed forever, *she* herself changed forever. Bad enough she'd had to rebuild her strength and confidence, her courage, her ability to sleep in a darkened room without feeling terror. Bad enough her body had been raped.

But *this* one, this animal, this son of a bitch in a different city three thousand miles away—he had done something even more malevolent. He had raped her mind.

That was it, what she hadn't wanted to face. A man had coolly and methodically studied the details of how her life had been destroyed, and then he had sickly replicated those details with precision. He had set out to violate her mind, to shatter it until the jagged pieces of it left her utterly helpless with terror, until she was no more than an insensible robot programmed to obey him.

He was ten times worse, a hundred times worse, than the man in Boston.

Though her eyes were now filled with hot tears of rage and acceptance, Dinah was immediately aware when Max came into the room. She didn't turn, but when he slipped his arms around her from behind she relaxed against him.

"More demons?" he asked gently, rubbing his cheek against her silky hair.

"The last one." Her voice was quiet, steady. "He did worse than use me, Max. He conned me. Tricked me. Without an ounce of compunction or mercy, he set out to destroy me. They don't even have a name for that, for what he did."

Max turned her to face him. His hands lifted to cup her face, the thumbs rubbing the wet traces of her tears. "But he didn't win, Dinah. He won't win."

She stared up at him, at the deceptively hard face and tender eyes of the man she loved, and for the first time she really began to accept her triumph. However painful the process had been, she was finally healed.

"I love you," she told Max intensely.

For a moment, he could barely breathe. Her eyes were clear finally, haunting now only in their luminous beauty, free of shadows, of the last tendrils of pain and fear.

It was what Max had been waiting for, hoping for, and he could hardly believe they had both won. His voice rough with emotion, he said, "Marry me, Dinah."

Her arms lifted to his neck, and her lips curved in a wondering smile. "Yes," she whispered. "Yes, Max, please."

The sun broke over the horizon just then, turning the bay to silver and bathing the two of them in brilliant light. But Max turned his back on the spectacular sunrise to carry Dinah back to their bed.

On Wednesday afternoon, the call came.

Nine

In the end, the trap was sprung with almost ridiculous ease. It was, Max said afterward, almost always the case when expectations were built to a fever pitch. They'd already had one letdown when they had realized that their assumptions had been wrong. It was only natural that the whole thing would end with a whimper instead of a bang.

Dinah had suspected as much when she'd received the call from her tormentor because, despite her earlier pang of fear, hearing that cruel, whispery voice had aroused nothing in her except a cold fury. It had, in fact, required all the acting skills she could summon for her to play the role of a terrified woman.

But by the time she obediently opened the same door as before just before midnight on Thursday, she had herself well in hand, and played her part perfectly. And if he thought it was fear rather than revulsion that caused her to shrink back when he slipped in past her, so much the better.

"The corridor alarms?" he hissed.

"Deactivated," she said dully, allowing the door to ease shut behind him. This particular corridor was dimly lit, and all she could see of him was that he was dressed head to toe in black, wore a ski mask, and carried both a small pouch of tools and a couple of large burlap sacks.

She was vaguely surprised. He wasn't very big, even though she had thought he was. When he had duplicated the circumstances of the rape, awakening her from a sound sleep by holding her down in the bed, she had been convinced that he, like the man who had raped her, was large and powerful. But he wasn't. He was of medium height and slender.

It was amazing how fear—and a carefully mapped-out duplication of a devastating attack—could shock the imagination into believing what wasn't real.

"What about the guards?" he demanded.

Dinah took a step back away from him, deliberately cornering herself, and letting rage shake her voice. "I told you how they patrol. One's in the East wing now, one in the—the West. They move clockwise and . . . and meet in the lobby once every hour."

He suddenly gripped her arm, his fingers tightening with a silent warning. "The door code?"

"This one is—six, seven, three," she whispered.

He released her and half turned, quickly punching the numbers into the keypad. The door opened easily, and he made a sound of satisfaction as he allowed it to shut again.

Dinah stood trembling, her eyes lowered because she was afraid he might see it was from anger rather than fear.

His gloved hand went to her chin and wrenched it upward. "Remember what I said, Dinah. You'll do exactly as I say, or I'll get to you. That fancy apartment of your boyfriend's has a cute security system, but he can't guard you twenty-four hours a day. I got to you in Boston, I got to you here. I'll do it again if you force me to."

Dinah's mind was cold and clear, but her voice shook obediently. "I will. Please—please just leave me alone. Don't hurt me again." The wire she was wearing would record all of this, and she hoped Max wouldn't have to listen to it. He was so strained by the risk she was taking now that it wouldn't require much to push him over the edge.

"I will if I have to, Dinah," he warned cruelly. "And this time, I won't leave you alive. Do you understand?"

"Yes," she whispered.

"Good. Very good." He stroked her cheek in an obscenely comforting touch. "Now go back to your office. Close the door, and don't come out for at least an hour. Then leave the museum just the way you always do, very calmly. If you do *exactly* what I say, you'll never hear from me again."

"I will." All of them had worried that he might decide to knock her out—or worse—but it was obvious he was convinced Dinah was completely under his control.

They had counted on that.

She walked beside her tormentor for several yards, then turned away from him silently and headed for the hallway of offices. She was afraid then, feeling the way any victim would with a dangerous animal at her back, out of her sight. Then she turned a corner, and Max was there.

He pulled her into his arms, both of them silent because they didn't know which way the thief had gone. He could have been close enough to hear them. Max held her tightly, and she could feel his heart thudding against hers.

It wasn't so much, what she'd done. But something could have gone wrong. That's what had haunted him—the risk that something could go wrong. Though it hadn't been spoken aloud, all of them knew that a man ruthless enough to use terror as his tool might not balk at murder.

They were silent until a shadow glided around the corner Dinah had just turned, and Wolfe spoke in a low voice.

"It's all right. One of the cops just reported he's

heading for the gem display three corridors over." Wolfe was holding a small transistor with an earpiece in place, and was listening to the muted conversations of the dozen police officers placed throughout the building. Though the conversation with Dinah was certainly damning, all of them wanted to catch this thief in the act of stealing.

Max looked down at Dinah, his hands lifting to frame her face. "Are you all right, sweetheart?"

She smiled at him. "I'm fine. Really. And when he's behind bars, I'll be perfect."

He kissed her, then kept one arm around her as he looked at Wolfe. "Is it who you thought?"

Wolfe hesitated, then clearly decided that Max wouldn't do something reckless now that they were so close to the end of things. He nodded. "Yeah, I got a good look at his size and build, as well as the way he moves. Name's Thornton. Philip Thornton. He runs an art gallery over on Bay Avenue."

Max stiffened. "Thornton. My God, I bought a painting from him last year."

"I was afraid you might have," Wolfe murmured. "Nice place for a thief to work, huh? The ironic thing is—he doesn't steal paintings. He likes gems."

Morgan joined them just then, her lovely face showing faint disappointment. "Hey, I thought we were in for an exciting night," she complained.

Max said, "It's been exciting enough for me, thank you."

"And me," Dinah agreed, removing the small listening device that was pinned just inside the lapel of her jacket and handing it to Wolfe.

Morgan smiled faintly, but looked at Wolfe with a pleading gaze that most men—even those favoring blondes—couldn't resist. "At least let me watch them collar him."

"Morgan—"

"Please?"

Wolfe sighed, then took her hand and began to

lead her away. Over his shoulder he said to the other two, "We'll let you know when the shouting's over."

Alone again, Dinah smiled up at Max. "I really am all right," she told him quietly.

Max drew a deep breath and released it slowly. "I don't ever want to risk you again," he said. "I don't ever want to lose you, Dinah."

Her eyes glowed with the brilliance he loved. "I think we both took the gamble of our lives. And I know we've won. Whatever happens in the future, we've won. I love you, Max."

"I love you too, sweetheart," he murmured, knowing she was right. They had gambled on each other.

And won.

There was one final thing Dinah felt she needed to do before she could begin to forget her tormentor: Face him. Face him in the light, where he no longer had the power to terrify. Face him when no mask protected him, when he had to look her in the eye, with both of them knowing what he had done to her.

Since he had been caught red-handed, condemning himself by taped evidence and numerous police eyewitnesses—with the museum's permission, the police had waited until the thief had broken two display cases before they had arrested him—it was likely the thief would plead guilty rather than go through the drawn-out process of a trial he would certainly lose. Because of that, Dinah doubted that she would face her tormentor across a crowded courtroom—and she was glad. Describing her ordeal in such an arena was something she preferred to avoid.

Besides that, she wanted to face him *now*, to end this chapter so she could get on with the rest of her life with Max. The police were agreeable, and Max knew it was something she had to do, so he didn't protest.

The lobby lights had been turned on, and the thief, his wrists secured with handcuffs behind his back, stood in a corner near the security guards' desk waiting for the police to take him away to be booked and jailed. The officer with him stepped several feet away as Dinah approached, giving her the privacy she had asked for, but the two of them remained under the steady observation of a half-dozen police officers as well as Max and Wolfe.

As she stopped slightly more than an arm's length from the thief, Dinah thought again how ordinary he seemed. Unmasked, his face was thin but not particularly hard, his eyes a muddy brown that looked, if anything, rather mild. But he smiled when she stood before him, and that evidence of amusement made her cold anger grow even stronger.

"Thornton. That's your name, isn't it? Philip Thornton?" she asked flatly.

"That's my name." His voice, no longer the eerie whisper, was as ordinary as the rest of him.

"Why did you do it? Why did you use me?"

He shrugged. "You were here. You had a weak spot."

Staring at him, Dinah realized that the man *was* soulless. He didn't see her as a person at all, but simply as a tool, a means to an end. She had known that intellectually, but facing him now the certainty was an emotional one as well. He would never feel even a single pang of remorse for what he had done to her—only regret that he had been caught.

Quietly, Dinah said, "I thought I'd feel different when I looked at you. That I'd want revenge, want to see you burn in hell. But, you know—I don't care what happens to you. You aren't worth another moment's thought."

As she turned away from the thief, her eyes and her thoughts were already fixed on Max. But everyone else watching the confrontation, the officers,

Max, and Wolfe, all noticed something she was unaware of.

Philip Thornton had stopped smiling.

Morgan felt more than a little charged by the events of the night, so even though it was nearly three in the morning she walked the four blocks to her home. She hadn't driven to the museum earlier. The others who did had parked in places other than the museum lot so as not to alert their thief.

It was a relatively safe neighborhood, the streets well lit and quiet at this time. Still, Morgan hadn't survived ten years on her own without learning not to take chances: She habitually carried both an ear-splitting police whistle on her keyring and a purse-size can of Mace. As she walked along briskly, she kept one hand in her purse and held the whistle ready in the other.

The precautions were routine, she felt neither nervous nor threatened by her surroundings. Her mind was occupied with thoughts of one successful, if disappointingly tame, capture of a thief just a few hours ago, and speculation about those thieves still at large.

She had a strong feeling that the weeks ahead would contain more than their fair share of tension and excitement. Both before and after the opening of Mysteries Past, there were sure to be interesting developments. She had a great deal of work ahead, especially with the security arrangements lagging badly. There would be more responsibility for her, too, unless she missed her guess. She doubted Max would wait much longer before carrying Dinah off on a honeymoon.

That suited Morgan just fine. She enjoyed responsibility. And she was looking forward to the possibilities of tension and excitement—even danger. With that gang of thieves still baffling the police, and

Quinn very likely making his presence felt in the city, this looked like the place to be.

"Good evening, Morgana."

She stopped dead in her tracks, her heart beating with an uneven rhythm. The walkway leading to her apartment building was just a few yards away on her left. She turned slowly to search out the corner of the building where the voice had come from but saw only trees and shadows. Then a piece of the darkness moved, stepping toward her. Without thinking, she crossed the lawn, and as she neared and her eyes adjusted to the dimness, she saw that he was once again wearing a ski mask—but it was rolled up from the bottom to reveal the lower portion of his face.

He had a strong jaw, she noted. And his mouth was beautifully shaped. Both sensitive and sensual, and curved with humor . . .

Coming to her senses, Morgan shook off her fascination. The man was a *thief*, for heaven's sake! When she reached him, she said, "I have a can of Mace in my hand, and I'm not hesitant about using it."

Quinn lifted both hands—ungloved—in a placating gesture and chuckled. "Believe me, Morgana, I have no doubt of that. The last thing I have any intention of doing is to rouse your quite impressive temper." His tone was the one she remembered so vividly—light, insouciant, and somewhat mocking.

"What the hell are you doing here?" she demanded. "If you mean to rob this building, you can be sure I'll tell the police *exactly* who did it."

"You cut me to the quick, *cherie*. Would I be so base as to despoil the home of my adored?"

"Very funny," she snapped. "Forget the Don Juan act, because I'm not buying it. As for just how low you'd sink, let me put it this way. I'd hate to have your nerve in a tooth."

His white teeth flashed in a brilliant smile as he laughed softly again. "Morgana, you are a delight."

She ignored what sounded like a sincere compliment, because she suddenly realized something. "How did you know I lived here?"

"Apartment three twelve," Quinn said lazily. "I followed you home a few days ago."

Morgan made a mental note to pay much more attention to her surroundings. He'd been near— probably unmasked—and she hadn't seen him. "Well, don't do it again," she ordered irritably. "In case you hadn't realized, I don't want to have anything to do with you."

"I'm crushed," he murmured, then added, "curiosity brought me here, Morgana. Why didn't you tell the police about my being in the museum the other night?"

Morgan hadn't expected to have to defend that decision to him, and cast about frantically before coming up with something that would be a sensible answer. "I told you at the time it sounded too damned unlikely to be believed. Besides, what you stole—what I *think* you stole—was nothing compared to what that gang walked out of there with. What does it matter, anyway?"

"As I said—curiosity." In an apologetic tone, he said, "I'm afraid I leapt to a conclusion. Hope springs eternal, you know. However, since you've made your feelings quite plain, I'll retreat to lick my wounds in private."

Morgan swore inwardly when she realized she didn't want him to leave just yet. "I told you to cut the act. In the first place, you're a thief, which is something I'm not at all in sympathy with. In the second place, I happen to be the director of an exhibit that must be calling to you like a siren song. And in the third place, any woman would need her head examined, by an expert, if she for one single minute believed anything you said."

He smiled. "Suppose I were to say it wasn't an act, Morgana. Suppose I denied any interest in Mysteries

Past, and assured you I am completely to be trusted."

"I wouldn't believe you," she said firmly.

"Very wise of you, Morgana. Very wise indeed."

She should have backed away when he took a step toward her. Or blew her whistle. Or removed the Mace from her purse and aimed it at him. However, she did none of these things. What she *did* was to lift her face in the most natural way, and melt into his arms as if she belonged there.

She felt his hand at her throat, warm and hard, felt the strength of his arms as he held her against him. His eyes gleamed down at her with a green fire even the darkness couldn't diminish. And then his mouth closed over hers.

It was a teasing kiss, without force, yet there was an underlying desire that ignited a shimmering heat deep inside her. She was barely conscious of letting go of the Mace so she could put her arms around his lean waist, and only dimly heard the jingle of the keys still dangling from her fingers. All she was really aware of was the hardness of his body against hers and the seduction of that kiss.

She felt dazed when he raised his head, and could only stare up at his shadowy face in silence. Her heart was pounding and her breathing was unsteady, and she couldn't think at all. He gently removed her arms from his waist and stepped back, releasing her completely. If he was feeling some effect from the embrace, it wasn't at all obvious. When he spoke, his voice sounded, if anything, amused.

"Don't forget me, Morgana."

It sounded like a final good-bye, and that impression intensified when he faded back into the shadows. Before she could regain command of her wits, he was gone.

Just as it had been in the museum, Morgan felt bereft, as acutely conscious of his absence as she had been of his presence. She wanted to call out his name, and it cost her a severe struggle not to.

Dammit, she didn't even *know* his name! All she knew was the infamous nickname of a conniving thief.

Standing alone in the darkness, Morgan berated herself silently, furious and chagrined at how easily—how maddeningly easily—he had managed to intrigue her mind and affect her body. It was a typically chilly San Francisco night, but she felt hot, and told herself it was from sheer embarrassment. She lifted a hand to tug at the high collar of her sweater, and then froze.

Her favorite piece of jewelry, the only piece of real value she owned, was a gold pendant she wore suspended on a fine gold chain. The pendant was heart shaped and encrusted with numerous small rubies.

And it was gone.

Morgan let out a small sound. Quinn, if he'd heard it, would have had no difficulty interpreting it. And the lively sense of self-preservation that had kept him alive and at large for ten years would have started warning bells jangling.

If he truly hadn't intended to rouse Morgan's considerable temper, he had failed wonderfully.

On Friday morning, Max leaned against the corner of Dinah's desk trying to entice her out of the office so that they could shop for an engagement ring. Since the engagement was short—only a week to be followed by a brief wedding ceremony, then a lengthy honeymoon—Dinah was protesting the need for a ring.

"Just one simple gold band is enough," she told him firmly.

"I want to give you a sapphire," he said. "And then, there's all the Bannister family jewelry."

"Your mother doesn't have that?"

Max shook his head. "When she and Dad divorced, she said that if she wasn't going to keep his name, she certainly wouldn't keep that stuff. It's been in storage for years." He smiled at her. "Meant for my wife."

Dinah returned the smile, but said wryly, "Maybe you'd better leave it in storage a little longer. Until a few more thieves are caught."

Max shrugged. "Sooner or later, the police will catch up to that gang—especially if they keep risking such large-scale operations. Security around everything of value in the city has been tightened."

"What about Quinn? Increased security never stopped him."

"We haven't heard a whisper of him since the night Morgan met him," Max replied calmly. "Maybe he's gone."

"He's still here." Morgan threw out the disgusted statement as she walked into the room. She sat down in a chair and scowled on them both. "At least, he was as of last night."

Max lifted an eyebrow. "How do you know?"

"Call it intuition." Morgan wasn't about to tell the truth. "And, besides—"

"Besides what?" Max was looking at her intently.

Morgan struggled with herself for a moment, then exploded. "That lousy, rotten, no-good thief *stole my necklace!* My only decent piece of jewelry, and he took it!"

"How did he do that?" Dinah asked.

Feeling herself blush, Morgan barely managed to hold on to her fierce expression. "He was waiting outside my apartment last night and . . . He distracted me, all right? My . . . my guard was temporarily down. Does it matter how he did it? The man has no scruples, no morals—and not much longer to live, because I'm going to kill him."

Max and Dinah exchanged glances, and then he said, "You'll have to get in line, Morgan."

She glared at them both for a moment, then got hold of herself. Standing, she squared her shoulders and gave herself a little shake as if to throw off thoughts of annoying cat burglars.

It was an impressive performance, but she spoiled it by saying somewhat wistfully, "Well, every woman should encounter a genuine scoundrel at least once in her life. It teaches her to appreciate decent men."

Epilogue

The worn folder contained a number of eight-by-ten color photographs, pictures that had been printed again and again in books and magazines all over the world. The Bannister collection rivaled the treasures of the Pharaohs in terms of sheer dazzling mystique and public fascination. It was the last great family collection of jewelry and artworks, privately owned and displayed only at the whim of its owner. It hadn't appeared publicly for more than thirty years.

He opened the folder with hands that weren't quite steady, and a tight little breath escaped him when the light of the desk lamp fell onto the first photograph. No matter how many times he saw it, the effect on him was always the same. Simply but exquisitely set in a pendant of twenty-four-karat gold, the Bolling diamond was breathtaking. It was a seventy-five-carat teardrop canary, the brilliant yellow hue so vivid it was as if the stone had captured a piece of the sun.

The centerpiece of the Bannister collection, it was flawless and priceless. Like the Hope diamond, the Bolling possessed a colorful and often tragic history; it was supposed to be cursed, but he didn't believe in curses.

He rubbed a finger across the photo, almost able to feel the coolness of the polished stone. Then, forcing himself, he turned the photo over and began briefly studying the others, one by one. Individually they had less of an effect on him than the Bolling had, but the splendor of the entire collection made his heart pound almost painfully.

The Black Royal diamond, forty carats, was a perfect oval surrounded by brilliant white diamonds; it had, supposedly, been a ransom payment for a kidnapping the history books never mentioned.

The Midnight sapphire, a two-hundred-carat square stone, flawed but beautiful in its rich, deep color. Legend had it that the stone—believed to be nearly a thousand years old—had been found, faceted and dully polished, in the ruins of a temple in India almost three hundred years before.

The Talisman emerald, a hundred and fifty carats of oval green fire engraved with cryptic symbols no one had yet been able to decipher, and set in a wide bangle bracelet of twenty-four-karat gold. In mystical circles, the story persisted that the emerald had been worn by Merlin, and had been used to amplify the wizard's powers.

There were also numerous lesser pieces of jewelry—lesser in terms of value, but each stunning. Necklaces, rings, and bracelets of gold set with cut and polished gems. From the brilliance of diamonds to the opacity of jade, ivory, and opal, virtually every precious and semiprecious stone known to man was represented at its very best.

In addition, there were figurines, cups, decanters, and religious works of art in gold and studded with gems. Each piece had a story or legend connected to it. Each piece was superb. Together, they would have tempted a saint.

He wasn't a saint. With trembling hands, he gathered the photographs and returned them to the folder. The exhibit would open in eight weeks, and was scheduled to run for only two months in San Francisco. After that, the collection would be returned to the safety and silence of the vaults that had protected it for decades.

Unless someone got to it first.

Author's Note

The idea for the *Men of Mysteries Past* series came to me some time ago, springing into my mind virtually full-blown and almost neon with energy—a rare occurrence, I promise you. It was a signal to me that I'd have a ball writing the stories, and that's exactly what happened.

You've now read the first story, *The Touch of Max*, which I hope you enjoyed. If you still have questions about some of the characters, don't worry—the story isn't over yet. Next is *Hunting the Wolfe*, in which Wolfe copes with a small, blond computer programmer who has a little blond cat, a fearless nature, and a few secrets.

And what about Quinn, you ask? Well, he's still in San Francisco, still on the loose—and Morgan hasn't seen the last of him. . . .

THE EDITOR'S CORNER

Next month LOVESWEPT salutes **MEN IN UNIFORM**, those daring heroes who risk all for life, liberty . . . and the pursuit of women they desire. **MEN IN UNIFORM** are experts at plotting seductive maneuvers, and in six fabulous romances, you'll be at the front lines of passion as each of these men wages a battle for the heart of the woman he loves.

The first of our dashing heroes is Brett Upton in **JUST FRIENDS** by Laura Taylor, LOVESWEPT #600—and he's furious about the attack on Leah Holbrook's life, the attack that cost her her memory and made her forget the love they'd once shared and that he'd betrayed. Now, as he desperately guards her, he dares to believe that fate has given him a second chance to win back the only woman he's ever wanted. Laura will hold you spellbound with this powerful romance.

In **FLYBOY** by Victoria Leigh, LOVESWEPT #601, veteran Air Force pilot Matt Cooper has seen plenty of excitement, but nothing compares to the storm of desire he feels when he rescues Jennifer Delaney from a raging typhoon. Matt has always called the world his home, but the redhead suddenly makes him long to settle down. And with wildfire embraces and whispers of passionate fantasies, he sets out to make the independent beauty share his newfound dream. A splendid love story, told with plenty of Victoria's wit.

Patricia Potter returns to LOVESWEPT with **TROUBA-DOUR,** LOVESWEPT #602. Connor MacLaren is fiercely masculine in a kilt—and from the moment she first lays eyes on him, Leslie Turner feels distinctly overwhelmed. Hired as a publicist for the touring folk-singer, she'd expected anything except this rugged Scot who awakens a reckless hunger she'd never dare confess. But armed with a killer grin and potent kisses, Connor vows to make her surrender to desire. You'll treasure this enchanting romance from Pat.

In her new LOVESWEPT, **HART'S LAW,** #603, Theresa Gladden gives us a sexy sheriff whose smile can melt steel. When Johnny Hart hears that Bailey Asher's coming home, he remembers kissing her breathless the summer she was seventeen—and wonders if she'd still feel so good in his embrace. But Bailey no longer trusts men and she insists on keeping her distance. How Johnny convinces her to open her arms—and heart—to him once more makes for one of Theresa's best LOVESWEPTs.

SURRENDER, BABY, LOVESWEPT #604 by Suzanne Forster, is Geoff Dias's urgent message to Miranda Witherspoon. A soldier of fortune, Geoff has seen and done it all, but nothing burns in his memory more than that one night ten years ago when he'd tasted fierce passion in Miranda's arms. When he agrees to help her find her missing fiancé, he has just one objective in mind: to make her see they're destined only for each other. The way Suzanne writes, the sexual sparks practically leap off the page!

Finally, in **HEALING TOUCH** by Judy Gill, LOVESWEPT #605, army doctor Rob McGee needs a wife to help him raise his young orphaned niece—but what he wants is

Heather Tomasi! He met the lovely temptress only once two years before, but his body still remembers the silk of her skin and the wicked promises in her eyes. She's definitely not marriage material, but Rob has made up his mind. And he'll do anything—even bungee jump—to prove to her that he's the man she needs. Judy will delight you with this wonderful tale.

On sale this month from FANFARE are four fabulous novels. From highly acclaimed author Deborah Smith comes **BLUE WILLOW**, a gloriously heart-stopping love story with characters as passionate and bold as the South that brought them forth. Artemas Colebrook and Lily MacKenzie are bound to each other through the Blue Willow estate . . . and by a passion that could destroy all they have struggled for.

The superstar of the sensual historical, Susan Johnson tempts you with **SINFUL**. Set in the 1780s, Chelsea Ferguson must escape a horrible fate—marriage to a man she doesn't love—by bedding another man. But Sinjin St. John, Duke of Seth, refuses to be her rescuer and Chelsea must resort to a desperate deception that turns into a passionate adventure.

Bestselling LOVESWEPT author Helen Mittermeyer has penned **THE PRINCESS OF THE VEIL,** a breathtakingly romantic tale set in long-ago Scotland and Iceland. When Viking princess Iona is captured by the notorious Scottish chief Magnus Sinclair, she vows never to belong to him, though he would make her his bride.

Theresa Weir, author of the widely praised **FOREVER**, delivers a new novel of passion and drama. In **LAST SUMMER**, movie star Johnnie Irish returns to his Texas hometown, intent on getting revenge. But all thoughts of getting even disappear when he meets the beautiful widow Maggie Mayfield.

Also on sale this month in the hardcover edition from Doubleday is **SACRED LIES** by Dianne Edouard and Sandra Ware. In this sexy contemporary novel, Romany Chase must penetrate the inner sanctum of the Vatican on a dangerous mission . . . and walk a fine line between two men who could be friend or foe.

Happy reading!

With warmest wishes,

Nita Taublib

Nita Taublib
Associate Publisher
LOVESWEPT and FANFARE

Don't miss these fabulous
Bantam
Women's Fiction
titles
on sale in JANUARY

BLUE WILLOW
by Deborah Smith

SINFUL
by Susan Johnson

PRINCESS OF THE VEIL
by Helen Mittermeyer

LAST SUMMER
by Theresa Weir

In hardcover from Doubleday,
SACRED LIES
by Dianne Edouard and Sandra Ware
authors of MORTAL SINS

BLUE WILLOW
by
Deborah Smith
author of MIRACLE

"Extraordinary talent . . . [BLUE WILLOW is] a complex and emotionally wrenching tale that sweeps readers on an intense rollercoaster ride through the gamut of human emotions." —*Romantic Times*

There had always been MacKenzies and Colebrooks at Blue Willow, their histories entangled like the graceful branches of the rare willow trees that thrived there. Artemas Colebrook had always loved the decaying estate in the lush hills of Georgia, but his soul was bound forever to the land the day the boy held tiny Lily MacKenzie minutes after her birth. Though he was torn from Blue Willow by the crumbling Colebrook fortune, Artemas swore that he would return someday—to Blue Willow . . . and to Lily.

A heartwrenching tragedy has brought Lily back to the tiny farm where she spent her childhood—a tragedy that has made Artemas's brothers and sisters her bitter enemies. Torn between family loyalties and their shared sense of destiny, Artemas and Lily must come to terms with a childhood devotion that has turned to bittersweet desire, a passion that could destroy all they have struggled for—even Blue Willow itself.

The following excerpt is an unusual one, but it gives a perfect introduction to young Artemas who grows up to become an absolutely wonderful hero in BLUE WILLOW. . . .

MacKenzie, Georgia, 1962

Artemas was only seven years old, but he knew a lot of secrets, most of them bewildering and terrible.

Uncle Charles had big balls and a tight ass. That was one secret. Father said so. Artemas must never again ask President Kennedy to arm-wrestle when the president was visiting at Uncle Charles's house, because it embarrassed Uncle Charles. Uncle Charles was the only Colebrook who'd inherited the Family Business Sense, and that was why Grandmother let him run the Colebrook China Company. She owned it but nobody asked her to do any work. That was another secret.

Father had married Mother for her money. Mother was half-Spanish, and Spaniards were Failed Royalty, whatever that was, but Mother was also, as Father put it, a Gold-Plated Philadelphia Hughs. What upset Father was that she'd done some mysterious bad things with money, and that had made Grandfather and Grandmother Hughs mad, so they'd stopped owning her, they'd Dis-Owned her, and her money had gone to Aunt Lucille, who'd married a Texas oilman and moved to a ranch, where people said she was raising children and hell.

Artemas loved Mother and Father desperately. That was no secret, but his love couldn't erase their frightening moods or the whispered words he'd heard once among the servants at Port's Heart, the home Grandfather Hughs had given them, by the ocean on Long Island.

The children will be marked for life.

Other secrets were trickier. No one told him they were secrets; he decided on his own. He'd rather die than reveal what he'd seen his parents do once in the gazebo at Port's Heart, after the bank men from New York drove away with boxes full of Father's important papers. Artemas, playing in the roses nearby, had been too frightened and horrified to let his parents know he was there.

Father and Mother had yelled at each other about money. Then Father tore Mother's skirt open and shoved her down on the gazebo's hard marble floor. Mother slapped Father, and Father hit her back until she screamed. Then he opened the front of his pants, got on top of her, and pushed down between her legs so hard that she began crying. He bumped up and down on her. Then he said, "You're as worthless as I am, you spoiled bitch."

The next day Mother cut up all her ball gowns with a pair of garden clippers. Then she bought new ones. There always seemed to be money for what Mother and Father wanted, particularly for clothes, parties, and travel. Father was on the board of Colebrook China, but Uncle Charles didn't ask him to do much, and he had plenty of free time.

The currents swirling around his family frightened Artemas. Only one place was safe from them.

Blue Willow. For the past two years Artemas had spent his holidays and summers there, with grand, dignified Grandmother Colebrook.

Blue Willow was a lost kingdom, with ruined outbuildings, dark forests, and overgrown fields to explore, and in the center was an enormous, echo-filled mansion perfect for a seven-year-old's fantasies, all hidden safely in the wild, watchful mountains of Georgia. Zea MacKenzie, the housekeeper, her husband, Drew, the gardener, and Drew's parents lived on their farm in the hollow beyond the mansion's lake and hills, along the ancient Cherokee trail. They were poor, Grandmother said, but they were MacKenzies, and that would always make them special.

Grandmother was special too. People whispered that when she was young she'd been something called a Ziegfeld Girl, before she became a Golddigger and married Grandfather. Grandfather had slipped and fallen out a window on Wall Street during the Depression, so to help Grandmother after he died, his sisters took Father and Uncle Charles away from her.

They told Grandmother she could stay at Blue Willow, and they'd raise her sons for her, in New York. She'd been at Blue Willow ever since. Which was fine with Artemas, because it meant he could visit her. Grandmother said he was her Consolation Prize, and he liked the sound of that.

But she was too old to keep up with a little boy all the time, so she turned him over to the wonderful MacKenzies. He loved them and felt loved by them in a way that made him feel frantic with guilt and confusion when he thought of his parents. Every day with the MacKenzies was an adventure. If being poor only meant that you had to live on a farm like theirs, he wanted to be their kind of poor.

The Colebrooks were poor now, too, but in a different way. They looked rich enough, but people felt sorry for them behind their backs. That was one of the secrets he must keep, Grandmother said.

Without money, all a Colebrook had was the Right Friends and an Important Name. Mother said that was enough, if you knew who to suck up to.

Artemas decided to avoid learning more family secrets if he could help it.

SINFUL
by
Susan Johnson
author of BLAZE and FORBIDDEN

"One of romance's hottest stars, Susan Johnson is in rare form in SINFUL, a highly sensual love story. . . . Titillating, scintillating, tension-filled and brimming over with heated love scenes . . . SINFUL is just that—sinfully enjoyable. Indulge yourself and your fantasies." —*Romantic Times*

Sweeping from 1780s Europe to the forbidden salons of a Tunisian harem, SINFUL tells the tale of a heroine determined to soil her reputation . . . and the noble rake who refuses to assist her.

Chelsea took a deep breath, looked out over the panorama of Cambridgeshire before her, returned her gaze to Sinjin's face, and quickly, before she lost her nerve, blurted out, "Would it be possible to consider this a business arrangement?"

"How much?" he presciently said with a faint smile, familiar with "business arrangements," beguiled by her sudden agitation. How charming she looked, blushing and flustered, riding bareback in a worn skirt and boy's jacket, her booted legs exposed with her skirt hitched up, one pink knee close enough to touch.

She inhaled and held her breath for a moment while he admired the fullness of her breasts constrained by the green velvet boy's coat. Then, exhaling in a great sigh, she admitted, "I can't say it."

"Fifty thousand?" he graciously suggested.

She glanced up sharply. "How did you know?"

"Your wager, darling. Obviously you're in need of fifty thousand."

"I'm not," she quickly interjected, "but my father is, you see," and then it all tumbled out—the eighty thousand he owed the money-lenders, the hopes to sell Thune if he won tomorrow, the deduction for that sale, then the remainder she was hoping she could raise from her . . .

"Business arrangement," Sinjin gently offered when she hesitated over the wording.

"I'd be ever so grateful," she added touchingly, and for the briefest moment, Sinjin considered giving her the money, as a gentleman would, without requiring her company for a week.

The brief moment passed, however, and more selfish motives intervened, having to do with the bewitching young lady short inches away, with rosy cheeks, golden wind-blown hair, an unearthly beauty, and a warm spirited nature that somehow seduced more boldly than the most celebrated belles of the Ton.

He would have her. On ungentlemanly terms. At any price.

"Would you like a down payment . . . now?"

"Oh no, I trust you."

Her words were so naive that he experienced a transient pang of conscience—quickly overcome. "In that case, consider the fifty thousand yours at next week's end."

"Thank you very much, Your Grace," she softly said. Her smile was angelic and dazzling at the same time, typical of the curious power she possessed to project both innocence and the most disarmingly opulent sexuality.

And at that moment, only heroic gentlemanly restraint—which proved, he thought, that he at least had a conscience, albeit infrequently used—kept him in the saddle. Of course, it would have been extremely embarrassing for him to stand at the moment, doeskin breeches more a second skin than enveloping raiment. "The pleasure's mine," he softly said with a certain degree of sincere feeling and smiled back at her.

Should she tell him she was flattered? Chelsea wondered, forcing back the chuckle that threatened to explode, aware of the Duke's arousal, equally aware of his unutterably beautiful smile that lit up his eyes, crinkled across his graceful cheekbones, tilted the corners of his mouth. Seductively.

"You're one flashy lad," she said with a grin, her gaze drifting downward suggestively. "Do you think you can wait a week?"

"Hell, no," he lazily drawled, his own grin in place. "Do I have to?"

She leaned back, propping herself on one elbow, looking very small on Thune's broad frame. "I'm verra tempted," she teased, dropping into a soft Scottish burr, her dark-lashed violet eyes traveling slowly down Sinjin's powerful body.

"Will Thune stay?"

At her nod, he threw a leg over Mameluke's neck, slid to the ground and, reaching up, lifted her off Thune. He didn't ask permission and she felt no constraint. His concern was obvious; in fact, he scanned the horizon with a minute scrutiny before taking her hand and leading her toward a small flat table rock. Initials had been carved in the soft sandstone by generations past, and he contemplated them with a brief distracted look before lifting her up and seating her.

"Tell me."

He shook his head. "Not for lady's ears."

"Do I look like a lady?" Chelsea retorted, piqued at being treated like a child.

Sinjin gazed at her for a long moment in her old tan serge skirt and short boy's jacket, his blue eyes as azure-luminous as the sky. "Oh yes," he said, low and husky. "Definitely. Absolutely. From a mile away."

His voice touched her like the summer sun, warmed her skin, heated her blood. His fingers stopped stroking her hands and curled protectively around them. "Are all Scottish lasses like you?" he whispered, his question tentative, inquiring beyond the simple query, for he wanted her like a schoolboy, without discipline or reason.

"Are all Sassenachs like you?" she whispered back, lifting her face for a kiss, feeling as he did . . . overpowered and out of control.

His mouth was smiling when he kissed her, and he murmured against the softness of her lips, "All the mamas hope not . . ."

But all the young ladies would be willing, Chelsea didn't doubt—mamas or not. And she swayed into the kiss, wanting to take what he offered.

He moved swiftly to steady her from falling, his hands gentle on her shoulders, and lifting his mouth, he murmured, "You ride the same way . . . recklessly."

"And fast," she softly replied, reaching for the buttons on his breeches.

"And wild . . ." He had the top three buttons on her jacket loose.

"And wild." She wanted him inside her, now, this instant; she wanted to feel the bliss, the hot, drenching rush of sensation.

He lifted her down then, for despite his carnal urgency, he

preferred a less exhibitionist position than atop a table rock on the crest of a hill visible for miles. Perhaps too he was protecting himself, an ingrained instinct for the most eligible bachelor in the kingdom.

The grass was soft, the huge sandstone monolith a shield from prying eyes, but Sinjin swiftly surveyed the surrounding landscape like a wolf scenting the wind before he returned his attention to Chelsea.

"There's no one about," she whispered, her jacket undone, her skirt flared out around her, a lush, nubile young maid fresh as spring green grass wanting him.

He recognized that look in a woman's eyes, that heated stage that ignored husbands or too observant servants, the kind that considered garden houses at breakfast routs sufficiently private. The kind that required he keep one foot against the door—which he was eminently proficient at. So he smiled his agreement instead of pointing out that someone could ride up from the far horizon in very short order. And reaching out, he brushed her opened jacket away from her breasts. "You're not cold." A hint of a smile played across his mouth.

"Au contraire," Chelsea whispered. She was so warm that the cool breeze was comfort to her bared flesh. Desire burned through her body. He had only to approach her and she wanted him; he had only to smile that slow lazy smile and she melted.

"Are you in a hurry?" He was asking how much time he had, but the lingering trail of his fingers circling her pink nipples distracted her, excited her, conferred a certain ambiguity to his query.

"Yes," she whispered, "and . . . no . . ." A small, languorous smile curved her lips, touched her eyes, lent a bewitching sensuality to the delicate beauty of her face. "And I hope you can accommodate both answers."

"With pleasure," he softly replied, "and beginning with the— yes . . ." he added, his dark lashes half-covering his eyes as he unbuttoned the remainder of the closings on his doeskin. "I'm at your service . . ."

PRINCESS OF THE VEIL
by
Helen Mittermeyer

We are proud to publish the first historical romance from one of your favorite LOVESWEPT authors!

"Intrigue, a fascinating setting, high adventure, a wonderful love story and steamy sensuality turn PRINCESS OF THE VEIL into a truly delicious summer treat. This is fine entertainment from a new voice on the [historical romance] scene." —*Romantic Times*

A proud Viking princess is pitted against a lusty Scottish chieftain in a duel of wits, courage, and passion. In the following scene, the Viking crew of her ship has just been overwhelmed by Scots when Princess Iona takes matters into her own hands. . . .

"'Tis my people's safety I would have," Iona called. "Swear by God that you'll grant this or I'll drive this sword through his skull."

After an endless moment, a bronze-haired man moved. Sword in hand, he strode into the water, then leaped up onto the Viking boat. Iona stood motionless, watching as he walked toward her along the oars.

"I am Sinclair," he said, and stepped onto the next oar. "It would seem you wish to be a warrior. Fight me then, Viking. If you win, your people go free. If I win . . ." He shrugged, and his hair glinted fire in the sun.

"Agreed," she said. "I'll pick up your gauntlet, Scot. 'Tis my right to choose the time and the weapons." She paused and stared at the giant, who was as comely as the devil. Then she smiled as the thrill of the challenge raced through her. "I choose now!" she suddenly shouted. "And oar running!"

Before the Scot could move, Iona jumped up into the air and landed hard on the oar where she'd been standing. Instantly, her feet began a running cadence that would keep the heavy oar straight and spinning. The object of oar running was to spin the oars until one person overbalanced and fell.

The Scot hesitated only a moment before he too jumped on his oar and began running. Iona watched him critically as she recalled every lesson she'd ever learned.

Long ago the perils and tricks of the sport had been drilled into her. A slap from the oars could break a limb or crack her skull; a misstep could send her crashing down on a spinning oar, maiming or killing her. She forced away those thoughts and concentrated on her other lessons—the speed needed to keep the oar parallel with the water, what would make it rise or fall, the best balance for using a weapon, when to strike, to feint, to back off. More times than she could count she'd been dumped in the frigid waters of BorgarFjord. But she'd struggled on until she'd mastered the skill, until she'd been able to stay on longer than some of the best Vikings, managing even to dunk them a time or two.

It took Iona only minutes to realize that her opponent had run the oars more than once. He was good, but not as good as she. He had strength, determination, and agility on his side, while she had the edge of her well-honed skill.

He often tried to reach her with the flat of his sword. She stayed just far enough away and speeded up, so that he'd have to do the same in order to prevent a collision of oars. If hers spun faster it would be atop his, giving her the advantage.

Magnus watched the Viking woman closely. She was damned good, and he hadn't expected that. Hell, he hadn't expected her to take up his challenge. She was a woman, outnumbered, her people's weapons down. But what a warrior she was. She looked as fragile as the silk that had been swathed around her head and now flew like a banner behind her. She was a beauty too. Silver and gold sparked her hair and skin, and her eyes were like the green leaves of summer, or like—

Damn! Her beauty had distracted him, and she'd almost toppled him. She was able to control her oar well. Ah! He could reach her. He tapped her backside with the flat of his sword, thinking to take her down, but she danced out of his way, her movements as sprightly as a nymph's. He'd get her, though. And maybe he'd keep her.

Iona saw the sudden dangerous glitter in his eyes and swore. The Scot might not intend to kill her, but he did intend to win. She had to do something soon, or he'd have her. There was one maneuver, perhaps unknown to him, that her father had called mortally perilous. Calling on the Holy Virgin, Christ, and Wotan, she made her decision.

She stared down at the whirling oar, counting every other beat. It had to be just right, or she'd break her leg.

"Wotan!" she shouted, and the age-old war cry was answered by her Vikings. Then she leapt high and came down hard on her opponent's oar. The landing jarred every tooth in her head, rattling through her like a blow. The instant her feet hit, she began running backward, the motion sending every muscle in her body screeching in pain and protest and wrenching a curse from her.

Could she hold on? Only if she'd caught him off guard enough, so that he couldn't bring his superior strength into play. Surprise flashed across his face, and she bore down with all her strength, spinning the oar as hard as she could.

The oar quivered, warning that the Scot was off balance. Pain spasmed in her back and neck as the Vikings roared behind her. They saw her advantage and sensed what she intended to do with it.

Iona increased her speed as she moved closer to him. Hefting the heavy sword, she swung it slowly, catching him on the arm. At the same moment, she jumped up and down, reversing once more, the action slamming through her head and body. The quick change sent the heavy oar splashing downward. She dug in, curling her toes around the wood. The Scot comprehended the ploy and fought for purchase, but he lost it.

Incredulity, fury, and stupefaction chased across his face as his sword flew from his hand. Then he spun in the air and fell backward into the sea.

The Scots cried out in anguish, and several men leapt up to grab his sword before it could follow him.

The Sinclair surfaced, and Iona easily saw both the anger and the vengeance in his eyes. "You win, Viking," he shouted up to her. "Your *people* shall be free. But *you* are my prisoner."

LAST SUMMER
by
Theresa Weir
author of FOREVER
and winner of two *Romantic Times* Awards

Set amid the glittering lights of Hollywood and the desert heat of Hope, Texas, LAST SUMMER is the emotionally powerful tale of a bad-boy actor and the beautiful widow who tames his heart. Driven out of his hometown, Hope, Johnnie Irish finds instant success in the movies and makes headlines with his outlandish behavior. When circumstances force him to return to Hope, he has revenge in mind. But all thoughts of getting even disappear when he meets local resident Maggie Mayfield.

In the following excerpt, Johnnie, who has volunteered to play the piano for a show Maggie is directing, threatens to leave in the middle of rehearsals.

"Are you saying if we had sex you'd stay?"

His anger softened a little, was replaced by an equally unflattering smugness. "That depends."

"On what?"

"On whether or not you're a good lay."

She'd never slapped anybody in her life. Until now, it had always seemed an immature and overly emotional thing to do. She raised a hand and swung. Hard.

His reflexes were quick. He blocked, his fingers locking around her wrist. The impact of the deflected blow sent a jarring vibration all the way up her arm to her shoulder socket.

"That's something you'll never know," she said through gritted teeth. "Whether I'm good or not. I want to go down in history as being the only woman in America you haven't screwed."

He laughed, but there was no humor in the sound. He was still holding her wrist high in the air. He pulled her close, his body slamming against hers, almost knocking the wind out of her. His other hand pressed against her lower spine. If anyone were to come in, it would look as though they were performing some bizarre dance.

"You're a self-righteous hypocrite," he said, his voice soft, threatening. In his eyes she read unshakable determination.

She tried to jerk away, but he held her fast. Suddenly his leg was behind hers, pushing at the back of her knees, making her fold. Her wrist slipped free of his grip. Arms behind her, she caught herself as her bottom hit the polished floor.

He dropped to his knees beside her, moving to cover her with his body. Before he could make contact, she scrambled backward across the floor.

His hand lashed out, grabbing her ankle, dragging her back to him.

"Let go of me! I hate you!" she screamed.

He pulled her underneath him. He held her down with his weight, forcing her legs apart, insinuating himself between her thighs.

She raised a hand to hit him once more. He grabbed it, stopping her. Off balance, they rolled until she was on top, her legs splayed on either side of his hips, her heaving breasts crushed to his rapidly rising and falling chest.

And as Johnnie stared up at her, he could see that her anger and hate were gone. Now there was only fear.

His own anger dissolved. He let go of her arms, closed his eyes, and let his head drop to the floor.

"Go ahead, hit me," he said, suddenly weary of the whole thing.

"W-what?"

"Hit me. I won't stop you this time."

Now that his eyes were closed, all of his senses were focused on his painful erection, throbbing against his zipper, against her warmth. Even without his eyes closed, he could remember how she felt. All soft. And warm. And wet.

Her weight shifted. She shoved herself upright, causing her pelvis to press against him even more, giving him even more of a pleasurable pain.

He groaned, just managing to keep his hands from cupping her bottom and grinding her into him. He had to have release. He'd never been in this kind of situation, where he couldn't get release.

Then her weight was completely gone, but he was still in agony. He flung an arm over his face, waiting for his body to calm down, his breathing to quiet, his muscles to relax.

Finally he opened his eyes.

She was standing a few feet away, her arms crossed at her chest, one leg straight, one hip out, her face flushed, hair hanging down her neck, having come loose from the band at the back of her head.

"Why are you leaving?" she asked.

He had to give her credit for trying to put things back on track. But damned if he'd tell her about Cahill and what had happened last night. It was too degrading. He just wanted to forget about it. He just wanted to get the hell out of Hope as fast as he could. "I told you, I'm bored."

"*When* are you leaving?"

"Right away. I'm driving to El Paso, then catching a flight to California." He needed to get going. He'd stayed too long already. Now that their wrestling match was over, the claustrophobic feeling he'd been fighting all day was coming back.

"What would make you stay?"

He didn't answer.

"Sex. Would you stay for sex?"

He drew in a breath, almost choking. "What?"

"You heard me. What if I told you I'd have sex with you if you stayed?"

He let out his breath. "Then I'd say you were bluffing."

She frowned.

But she was right about one thing. He wanted her. He'd like to have her at least once before he left.

He shoved himself to his feet and faced her. He didn't understand it, but he suddenly had the urge to touch her, not in a sexual way, but a comforting way. Just for the sake of touching her.

"If we ever do make love," he said, silently moving toward her, "it will be because you want to, and I want to."

He did touch her then, a palm to the side of her blood-warm face. Surprisingly she didn't move away. She simply stared at him, lips parted. He couldn't resist. He kissed her. Not a soft, gentle kiss, but a possessive kiss, his tongue quickly outlining her lips before plunging inside to stroke the wetness of her mouth. Her breasts were pressed to his chest. He could feel the hardness of each nipple, feel himself rising again, straining against the seam of his jeans.

One hand came down to cup her bottom. He lifted her into him, making sure she could feel him. Then he pulled his mouth from hers. "I'll stay," he told her, staring into her wide amber eyes. "But not because of some bargain."

He couldn't help but feel a twinge of self-mockery. His present attitude toward sex was a little different from the one he'd had only a month ago. And he supposed he should give Maggie credit for that.

She was still watching him, still pressed to him, one hand gripping his shirtsleeve, her eyes full of confusion and a sort of bemused wonder.

He kissed her again. Quickly this time, before he was tempted to pull her to the floor and make love to her so she wouldn't forget him.

He could put up with Hope, Texas, for three more days. And three more nights. He would survive the nightmares. The tossing and turning and trying to forget. He would do it for Maggie.

OFFICIAL RULES TO WINNERS CLASSIC SWEEPSTAKES

No Purchase necessary. To enter the sweepstakes follow instructions found elsewhere in this offer. You can also enter the sweepstakes by hand printing your name, address, city, state and zip code on a 3" x 5" piece of paper and mailing it to: Winners Classic Sweepstakes, P.O. Box 785, Gibbstown, NJ 08027. Mail each entry separately. Sweepstakes begins 12/1/91. Entries must be received by 6/1/93. Some presentations of this sweepstakes may feature a deadline for the Early Bird prize. If the offer you receive does, then to be eligible for the Early Bird prize your entry must be received according to the Early Bird date specified. Not responsible for lost, late, damaged, misdirected, illegible or postage due mail. Mechanically reproduced entries are not eligible. All entries become property of the sponsor and will not be returned.

Prize Selection/Validations: Winners will be selected in random drawings on or about 7/30/93, by VENTURA ASSOCIATES, INC., an independent judging organization whose decisions are final. Odds of winning are determined by total number of entries received. Circulation of this sweepstakes is estimated not to exceed 200 million. Entrants need not be present to win. All prizes are guaranteed to be awarded and delivered to winners. Winners will be notified by mail and may be required to complete an affidavit of eligibility and release of liability which must be returned within 14 days of date of notification or alternate winners will be selected. Any guest of a trip winner will also be required to execute a release of liability. Any prize notification letter or any prize returned to a participating sponsor, Bantam Doubleday Dell Publishing Group, Inc., its participating divisions or subsidiaries, or VENTURA ASSOCIATES, INC. as undeliverable will be awarded to an alternate winner. Prizes are not transferable. No multiple prize winners except as may be necessary due to unavailability, in which case a prize of equal or greater value will be awarded. Prizes will be awarded approximately 90 days after the drawing. All taxes, automobile license and registration fees, if applicable, are the sole responsibility of the winners. Entry constitutes permission (except where prohibited) to use winners' names and likenesses for publicity purposes without further or other compensation.

Participation: This sweepstakes is open to residents of the United States and Canada, except for the province of Quebec. This sweepstakes is sponsored by Bantam Doubleday Dell Publishing Group, Inc. (BDD), 666 Fifth Avenue, New York, NY 10103. Versions of this sweepstakes with different graphics will be offered in conjunction with various solicitations or promotions by different subsidiaries and divisions of BDD. Employees and their families of BDD, its division, subsidiaries, advertising agencies, and VENTURA ASSOCIATES, INC., are not eligible.

Canadian residents, in order to win, must first correctly answer a time limited arithmetical skill testing question. Void in Quebec and wherever prohibited or restricted by law. Subject to all federal, state, local and provincial laws and regulations.

Prizes: The following values for prizes are determined by the manufacturers' suggested retail prices or by what these items are currently known to be selling for at the time this offer was published. Approximate retail values include handling and delivery of prizes. Estimated maximum retail value of prizes: 1 Grand Prize ($27,500 if merchandise or $25,000 Cash); 1 First Prize ($3,000); 5 Second Prizes ($400 each); 35 Third Prizes ($100 each); 1,000 Fourth Prizes ($9.00 each) ; 1 Early Bird Prize ($5,000); Total approximate maximum retail value is $50,000. Winners will have the option of selecting any prize offered at level won. Automobile winner must have a valid driver's license at the time the car is awarded. Trips are subject to space and departure availability. Certain black-out dates may apply. Travel must be completed within one year from the time the prize is awarded. Minors must be accompanied by an adult. Prizes won by minors will be awarded in the name of parent or legal guardian.

For a list of Major Prize Winners (available after 7/30/93): send a self-addressed, stamped envelope entirely separate from your entry to: Winners Classic Sweepstakes Winners, P.O. Box 825, Gibbstown, NJ 08027. Requests must be received by 6/1/93. DO NOT SEND ANY OTHER CORRESPONDENCE TO THIS P.O. BOX.

Women's Fiction

On Sale in January

BLUE WILLOW

29690-6 $5.50/6.50 in Canada

☐   **by Deborah Smith**

Bestselling author of MIRACLE

"Extraordinary talent.... A complex and emotionally wrenching tale that sweeps the readers on an intense rollercoaster ride through the gamut of human emotions." —<u>Romantic Times</u>

SINFUL

9312-5 $4.99/5.99 in Canada

☐   **by Susan Johnson**

Author of FORBIDDEN

"The author's style is a pleasure to read and the love scenes many and lusty!" —<u>Los Angeles Herald Examiner</u>

PRINCESS OF THE VEIL

29581-0 $4.99/5.99 in Canada

☐   **by Helen Mittermeyer**

"Intrigue, a fascinating setting, high adventure, a wonderful love story and steamy sensuality." —<u>Romantic Times</u>

LAST SUMMER

56092-1 $4.99/5.99 in Canada

☐   **by Theresa Weir**

Author of FOREVER

"An exceptional new talent...a splendid adventure that will delight readers with its realistic background and outstanding sexual tension." —<u>Rave Reviews</u>